STOLEN AWAY

STOLEN
AWAY

Christopher Dinsdale

Napoleon

Toronto, Ontario, Canada

Cover art by Christopher Chuckry

Napoleon Publishing
Toronto, Ontario, Canada

Le Conseil des Arts | The Canada Council
du Canada | for the Arts

Napoleon Publishing acknowledges the support of the Canada Council for our publishing program.

Printed in Canada

10 09 08 07 06   5 4 3 2 1

Library and Archives Canada Cataloguing in Publication

Dinsdale, Christopher, date-
          Stolen away / Christopher Dinsdale.

ISBN 1-894917-20-0 (pbk.)

          1. Irish--Newfoundland and Labrador--Juvenile
fiction. 2. Beothuk
Indians--Juvenile fiction.   I. Title.
PS8607.I58S76 2006   jC813'.6   C2006-903891-0

For the wonderful women
in my life:
my wife, Amanda,
my mom,
and my daughters
Sarah, Johanna and Stephanie

Acknowledgements

I would first like to thank Amanda, my wife, for her continued support during the many hours in which I'm huddled in my basement burrow, spilling my imagination onto the laptop computer. I would also like to thank my family, friends, colleagues and students who, with their enthusiasm for *Broken Circle*, encouraged me to continue my writing. I can't put into words how much I appreciate the kind thoughts. Special mention also goes to my Grade Five student, Anna, who thought up the title, *Stolen Away*. I would also like to thank Newmarket Public Library for their wonderful collection of reference materials as well as their enthusiastic support for each one of my books. The New Brunswick Museum and the Newfoundland Museum were very helpful in answering the many questions I had regarding the history of the Vikings in North America. I thank those institutions for their time and patience.

This novel is based on ancient Irish legends, Norse sagas and what little we know of the Beothuck people. The storyline itself is straight from my own imagination, therefore the plot and characters (except for Thorfinn Karlseffni, the Viking leader) should not be taken for historical fact.

Enjoy the adventure!

- Christopher Dinsdale

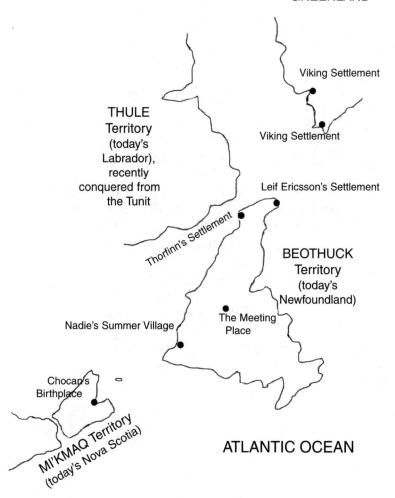

GREENLAND

Viking Settlement

THULE
Territory
(today's
Labrador),
recently
conquered from
the Tunit

Viking Settlement

Leif Ericsson's Settlement

Thorfinn's Settlement

BEOTHUCK
Territory
(today's
Newfoundland)

Nadie's Summer Village

The Meeting
Place

Chocan's
Birthplace

MI'KMAQ Territory
(today's Nova Scotia)

ATLANTIC OCEAN

Places in this book

ONE

Kiera ran her calloused fingers over the ancient grooves of the Stone. Cool and rough to the touch, its comforting texture reached into her soul and caressed her hidden anguish. She did not feel the tear that trickled down her cold cheek. Perched upright in the soft meadow earth, the table-sized rock was decorated with intricate patterns of ancient symbols and geometric crosses. The beautiful detail whispered words of comfort, whispers in a language that had not graced her ears since she had been kidnapped a lifetime ago. The Stone never failed to bring her a sense of fleeting tranquillity, even when she was in the gloomiest of moods.

Smiling through the tears, she glanced down at the intricately-carved pendant she was wearing around her neck. Shaped in the traditional Celtic cross, Kiera's only piece of jewellery and her single reminder of her past life, had an uncanny resemblance to the Stone itself, both in style and workmanship. The woven geometric markings of her pendant triggered memories of ghostly images. Warm embraces. Soft music. Laughter.

Love. They were so long ago, the memories of her early childhood, that they simply fluttered in and out of her thoughts. She tried to grab hold of them and live within them, if for only a moment, but like the butterflies that zigzagged past her in the breeze, they vanished far too quickly. Sadly, she realized that her memories were becoming as worn as the weathered grooves within the Stone itself.

She shook her head and focused again upon the markings of the Stone. It had been set here, in this meadow, for a reason, placed so its engravings pointed east towards the thundering ocean and the rising face of the sun. Why was it placed here? Could the Stone be some sort of marker? How was it possible that her ancestors had carved this beautiful design in a location that was a world away from her homeland?

As she so often did, she closed her eyes and imagined the small Celtic craft and the brave Irish mariners appearing on the eastern ocean horizon. Using the power of their small single sail, they would ply the waters to return to this windswept meadow and their ancient marker. Coming ashore, the mariners would see her waiting by the Stone, their faces lighting up in recognition of their similar descent. She would run into their arms and they would embrace her, the warmth of their common blood penetrating her cold, ocean-blown skin. Then, their mission complete, they would lead her to their boat, and together they would make the long eastward journey home.

Home.

Her dreamy thoughts were shattered by a low

animal-like moan from a Viking horn, echoing through the afternoon breeze. Jumping to her feet, she glanced at the angle of the sun and realized that she was in trouble. Thorfinn, the village leader, was beckoning everyone to return to the village. She glanced down at the basket by her feet. There were barely enough blueberries to cover the weaved bottom, and it was supposed to be full by now.

Crouching and crawling, Kiera quickly worked her way through grass and wind-bent bushes of the meadow, grabbing any low-lying blueberries within reach as she went. As she made her way awkwardly over the bush-covered rise, the Viking settlement came into view. Nestled in a gentle valley, the low, rectangular mud and thatch buildings, stables and pasture embraced the gentle curve of a meandering river.

Kiera quickly realized why Thorfinn had blown the alert. The river was teeming with splashing people. Every man, woman and child from the settlement was thrashing and stumbling in what looked like a maddened frenzy, lowering baskets and large pieces of cloth into the glistening water and hauling out magnificent fish moments later. As they threw the fish up onto the muddy embankment, several of the men scurried and slipped between the growing number of prized catches. With one swing of an iron rod, they clubbed the life out of their catch, then threw the flaccid bodies onto a growing pile at the edge of the meadow grass. It was the moment the settlers had been waiting for all summer. The salmon run had begun!

Kiera burst into a stumbling sprint. Thankfully, she would not have to worry about her lack of berries today. No one would notice that she had shirked her duties, since the excitement of the returning salmon would consume the thoughts of every villager. Kiera joined in with her own whoops and cheers as she launched herself, boots and all, into the creek. The water was frothing with life as thousands of fish tried to push their way upriver towards their ancestral spawning grounds. She laughed as a larger fish boldly tried to sprint between her leather boots. Pinning the creature with her ankles, she bent down and grabbed the fish through the gills. With one smooth motion, she flung the fish into the air and towards the waiting men on the shore.

"It's about time you showed up."

A strong hand grabbed her shoulder. Kiera spun around and looked into the squinting, sea-cragged eyes of her master, Bjorn. His huge body and etched face were fierce, but behind the menacing stare lay a sparkle of kindness in the knowing, blue eyes.

"I was out picking blueberries as Dagmar had asked," she said, defensively.

"Aye, and I saw your basket on the grass. Spent maybe twenty minutes of your two hours picking, I reckon. Daydreaming at the Stone again?"

Kiera didn't answer. She didn't have to. Her blushing cheeks gave her away once again. They were the bane of her existence.

His stare narrowed. "Well, since you've already had your break, you're not leaving this creek until you've hauled out more salmon than any other man, woman or child of the village. Understand?"

"Yes, sir," she answered, meekly.

As her master ordered, Kiera hauled out fish after fish without a break. The enthusiasm of the moment quickly waned. Even at dusk, when most of the villagers had returned to their homes to prepare for dinner, she stubbornly stayed in the creek until it was dark. She could no longer see the fish, but her other heightened senses could hear the approaching splashing and the movement of water against her legs. More often than not, her fingers would somehow find the slippery scales, then the gills of a salmon.

The sound of joyous feasting began to mingle with the splashing of the fish. The delectable aroma of grilled salmon drifted across the water. Her grumbling stomach urged her to follow the aromatic trail to its source. Kiera, however, willed herself to go on, knowing that she had not been given the permission to quit. Bjorn was not a cruel man, but it was simply not her way. Her master had told her to haul fish, and she would continue do so without question.

It was well into the evening when Bjorn appeared with his hands on his hips by the creek's edge. He had to duck as a rather large fish sailed by his head and landed on the grass behind him.

"I hope that was not intentional," he said in a half-serious manner.

She looked up, shocked at the voice. "I'm sorry! I didn't see you standing there."

He chuckled. "I think you've made up for your relaxing afternoon." He reached out a hand. "Come on."

Kiera smiled wearily as she took his hand, amazed that her numb legs still obeyed her commands. Kiera's teeth chattered as her boots sloshed towards the glowing sod homes. They paused as Bjorn effortlessly lifted a massive log up from the pile of stacked firewood, then carried it towards the doorway of the largest building and the waiting hearth beyond. Kiera never stopped marvelling at Bjorn's strength. She had once seen him lift a sick cow off the pinned leg of a fellow farmer. The man, she was sure, had strength that could rival a Norse god.

Bjorn and Kiera ducked under the low frame of the doorway. Kiera suppressed the urge to cough as the air suddenly became heavy with smoke and festive bantering. Bjorn threw the massive piece of wood into the crackling hearth, walked past two families feasting on fish, then stopped at a gathering in the far corner of the shelter. Kiera sat down heavily on a wooden stump, shivering. She was immediately attacked from behind by a tiny set of arms and a high-pitched squeal.

"Kiera! Kiera! You're back!"

Kiera reached back, pulled the little assailant over her head, upside down, and flipped the young girl onto her lap. Two huge blue eyes looked up at her with excitement. Bouncing, she waved a half-eaten piece of fish in one hand.

"Isn't it the most wonderful thing you have ever tasted?" she said, in awe. "This is my eleventh piece. Mama said I could have as much as I wanted. I've never had as much as I wanted, unless I'm with you when we're blueberry picking. Oops! I'm sorry, Kiera. I wasn't supposed to say that. Mama, you didn't hear that!"

Smiling, Kiera shook her head at her young friend's exuberance and looked over at the tall, blonde woman sitting next to her. Her beautiful hair had been loosely braided and hung almost to her waist. Her shoulders were covered with a wool cloak. Something moved within the cocoon she held against her chest. The soft, smacking sound of a contented nursing baby could be heard above the din of the noisy feast. She smiled, reached out tenderly and caressed Kiera's cheek.

"You're frozen. I hope Bjorn wasn't too hard on you."

Keira shook her head but grimaced as she tried to wiggle her frozen toes. "No. I deserved it. I should have picked more berries."

Dagmar looked down at her daughter. "Lorna, get Kiera her dinner."

Lorna bounced over to the fire and picked up a wooden pallet piled high with salmon and potatoes. She merrily skipped it back to Kiera.

Dagmar nodded at the food. "I saved this for you. Enjoy."

Kiera pinched a chunk of steaming pink salmon and placed it in her mouth. Her first chew released a flavor so wonderful that her entire body tingled in delight. Meanwhile, Dagmar had separated herself from the infant, who was now slung over her shoulder. After several pats, the baby produced a belch that seemed impossibly large for such a small person. Dagmar smiled and gently rocked the baby into a deep sleep.

Lorna tugged on Kiera's skirt. "Did you remember?" she asked, batting her long lashes.

Kiera shrugged. "Remember? Was I supposed to remember something?"

"Your surprise! You said you would have a surprise!"

"Oh, yes," Kiera smiled, winking at Dagmar. "The surprise. I remember now."

She reached under her wool cape and pulled out a small sack. Lorna gasped in excitement.

"Go ahead. Open it."

As if it were the most valuable present in the whole world, Lorna carefully pulled apart the top of the pouch and a grin broke across her face.

"Raspberries!"

"I found a small stand of raspberries near the edge of the river. Not enough for a family, but just enough to surprise a very sweet, young girl."

Lorna turned. "Mama, can I share them with my friends?"

"Go ahead. But it will be bedtime shortly."

"Thank you, Mama!"

Dagmar reached out to Kiera. "Thank you."

"My pleasure."

Together they watched Lorna and her friends chattering excitedly while they sampled the sweet treasure. Kiera took another bite of her salmon and let her eyes drift to the far door and the darkness beyond. "When I'm out there in the meadow, sometimes I'm overwhelmed by the beauty of this land. The flowers. The food. The endless forests. It's like a paradise, when you compare it to what we left behind in Greenland."

"Yes," said Dagmar, sighing, "but it is a paradise already claimed."

Kiera frowned. "The skraelings."

Dagmar nodded. "Although it has been over two months since their last raid, I fear that we will soon see them again."

"I understand the concern of the parents regarding the children's safety, but I feel so sorry for Lorna and the others, not being able to run free in these beautiful surroundings. The meadow in full bloom is almost magical. The children should be out there picking flowers, rolling down the hills, playing games..."

Kiera's voice drifted away, as misty images of such games floated into her mind from another life, an earlier life, a life of carefree joy and happiness. Her skin once again grew cold. She shook her head in an attempt to clear her thoughts. She was now a member of the Svensson family, a slave but treated more like an eldest daughter. She knew Dagmar and Bjorn cared for her deeply. There was no point in thinking about the past.

Dagmar didn't notice Kiera's longing gaze, looking instead at Lorna in the distance.

"You know that's impossible. We don't know what the skraelings would do to our children should they ever meet or capture one. For their own safety, we must keep them within the village."

"I understand," said Kiera, "but it is still a shame."

Dagmar nodded. "Bjorn understands that, too. That's why the elders are gathering tonight in order to discuss the details of another expedition."

"An expedition? To where?"

"To the southwest. They are hoping to find another land that is just as fertile as here but without the skraelings, or at least with skraelings that are not as hostile as our northern neighbours."

Kiera's eyes widened. "Do you mean we'll have to move? Again? We've only been here for two years."

"It simply is not safe here. The skraelings are becoming bolder and more dangerous with each raid. They are not going to leave us alone until we are gone. We have already lost Gardar and Erik to their arrows and harpoons. We must do something before we lose everything."

Kiera sighed. After two years of back-breaking work, the village was just starting to feel like a settled community.

"But moving further southwest will take us further away from your homeland."

Dagmar frowned. "That is true. We will be more isolated than ever. But as you said, these lands are plentiful and much more fertile than Greenland, which would be our only other option if we were to move again."

The thought of going back to Greenland sent mixed emotions tingling through Kiera. It was a barren wasteland, but it also gave her a ray of hope for the future. It was that much closer to her own homeland of Ireland.

"But what about the Stone?" asked Kiera.

"Ah, yes. the Stone was certainly a good omen. After our repairs at Leif's abandoned winter lodging, we found the Stone after a week's sail south. Seeing the Stone, we knew that we were in territory that had been previously explored by the Ancients. Our people have seen the same stones throughout northern Europe, Iceland and Greenland. We knew that if the Ancients had landed here and settled long enough to carve the Stone, then it would likely be a good place for us to land and settle as well."

Kiera was confused. "Why were the Ancients able to live here in peace and not us?"

Dagmar shrugged and laid the sleeping baby down on a thick blanket of rabbit fur. "Perhaps things are different now. Perhaps there were no skraelings, or they were on friendlier terms with the Ancients. It's hard to say what exactly has changed since that time long ago. If the Ancients had the same problems with the skraelings as we do today, then I doubt they would have had the time to carve such an impressive stone."

Kiera tried to rub the smoke out of her eyes. The heavy air always made her feel tired after a long day in the sun. Dagmar called for Lorna and arranged the furs into a bed on the wood slats that ran the length of the longhouse.

"It's time to go to sleep. There's no point waiting up for the men. They'll be singing and telling sagas long into the night."

Kiera laughed as the deep, burly chorus to a

well-known Odin legend rumbled through the darkened night. It was a warm, late summer evening. To further heat up the longhouse would be a waste of winter wood, so Kiera walked over to the hearth and helped douse the flames with piles of ash. The embers would keep until morning. The room was plunged into darkness, and a refreshing evening breeze swirled through the sod building.

Kiera was exhausted. Her body ached from the hard labour, but she didn't complain. Her belly was full, and her heart was warmed by the tiny hand that grabbed hold of her hair as Lorna's body curled up next to hers. She caressed the little girl's back. Life could be much worse, she thought to herself. She had a family who cared deeply for her. She was the adopted big sister of this little girl. In the villages of Iceland and Greenland, she had heard of almost unimaginable horror stories from other captured young women. The thought of what those girls had endured had kept her up many nights, and during those moments, she would utter a prayer of thanks for her situation. The whole village, in fact, was like one family. There was no choice. Without such a tight-knit community and full cooperation, survival in such a distant, foreign land would have been impossible. They were, in the truest sense, alone in another world. No one else within a month's sail cared whether they lived or died.

TWO

Kiera wasn't sure how long she had been sleeping when she was wakened by the bleating of a frightened sheep. She blinked in the absolute darkness. Silence. Must have been a dream, she thought, and rolled over. The bleating began again. And then...crackling. Something was wrong. How late was it? From the snoring on the far side of Dagmar, she knew that the meeting had ended and Bjorn had returned. She reached over Dagmar and shook the large shoulders of her master.

"Bjorn," she whispered, "wake up. I think something is happening outside."

Bjorn immediately sat up. It never ceased to amaze Kiera that regardless of how little sleep or how much drink Bjorn had consumed, he could somehow rouse himself in an instant. The crackling continued, and a cow now joined in the chorus of uncharacteristic sounds. Kiera heard him slip his dagger out from under his pillow. Moving catlike through the longhouse, he stopped in the centre and lightly clanked his dagger against the rock of the hearth three times. Dagmar then heard the rustling of covers, followed by the snapping on of leather armour and the gentle tinkling of metal as spears, swords and axes were quietly gathered. The men, as a unit, stepped carefully to the low doorway.

Kiera was surprised that she could see their faint outlines at the doorway, since there should have been no light on this moonless night. It was then that she knew something must be wrong. The light against the men's skin and armour flickered with a dangerous orange glow. The Viking warriors screamed with anger and horror as they burst out into the night. What followed was pure pandemonium.

The enraged yelling woke every sleeping infant in the village. The women began to shriek in panic from the confusion, the darkness only adding to their terror. Dagmar had her hands full with her howling baby while Lorna, shivering, clung to Kiera like a limpet.

"Come, Lorna. We must help the adults. You're a big enough girl to help me, right?"

Lorna nodded, confused and sleepy.

"Good girl. Come with me. We have to get the fire going."

Together, they crawled to the centre of the longhouse.

"Stay right beside me, Lorna, but don't touch anything. The embers are still very hot."

Kiera grabbed a log and scraped away the thick layer of ash from the hearth. The faint glow of still-warm embers gave her just enough illumination to find bits of kindling. She quickly piled them on top of the embers. Taking deep breaths, she began to blow life back into the hearth. A small fire caught and, with the addition of several logs, the fire began to crackle and roar.

The women and children, huddled together in their various family groupings, looked to Kiera with terrified eyes but nodded their thanks. The light seemed to make what was happening outside just a little less frightening.

"Go back to your mama, Lorna."

"But I want to stay with you!" she pleaded.

"Do as I say." The tone in Kiera's voice was not to be questioned. Lorna let go of Kiera and ran to the lap of her mother at the far end of the longhouse.

Kiera made her way to the doorway. She crouched down beside the frame and looked out. What she saw was a scene that would be fitting for a fevered nightmare. The livestock stable was ablaze with such ferocity that the entire village was illuminated by the frenzied flames. There were the shadowy outlines of sheep and cattle wandering between the buildings. She sighed with relief at the sight of the animals. The men must have freed them in time. Without the animals, the village would have been doomed. Among the buildings, she could see men chasing men, screaming and shouting. Swords were swinging and projectiles flew through the air. It was chaos.

A figure ran towards their building. Kiera was glad that someone was returning. She wanted to know what was happening and if there was anything that she could do to help. She noticed something strange, however, about the silhouette that was quickly approaching. His upper body was completely naked, and in his hand was a long pointed stick that she had never seen used by the Vikings. It was a skraeling!

Kiera spun away from the door and pressed her back against the inside of the log frame. What should she do? Kiera scanned the corner in which she stood. Everything was set up for the morning ritual of making bread. The stone quern for grinding the flour sat next to the wooden kneeding trough and iron baking plate.

A terrifying scream pierced the inner sanctuary of the longhouse. A short, broad-shouldered man leapt into the entranceway. His eyes burned with anger, feeding on the frightened screams of the women and children. Black lines, etched around his eyes and streaked along his cheek like the wings of a mighty bird, added to his nightmare appearance. In one hand, he held a bloody spear. He raised it, choosing his target. He took a step towards Ingrid, who, wide-eyed and frozen in fear, held her three young children to her waist.

His second step never touched the ground as the iron baking plate crashed into his stomach, doubling him over. Kiera heaved on the long, metal handle, raising the impromptu weapon above her head, then brought it crashing down hard onto the back of his skull. With a grunt, the intruder collapsed face-first onto the ground before her feet.

The entire building went quiet. The women stood together and simply stared at their prostrate attacker. Kiera didn't hesitate. She grabbed him by the legs and dragged him away from the entrance and into the corner of the building. She returned to the door, checked outside, then looked back towards the families. She nodded at the woman whose life she had just saved.

"Ingrid, we need rope."

A minute later, Ingolf, Ingrid's husband, arrived back at the longhouse, limping badly.

"We just chased the last one away. Is everyone well?"

Then he saw Kiera and Ingrid, with their knees on the skraeling's back, finishing off the final knots.

His jaw dropped. "What happened?"

"Kiera just saved your family—with this." Ingrid held up the baking plate.

Ingolf's expression went from shock to a relieved smile. "Thank the gods. And thank you, Kiera. How did you manage that?"

She shrugged, modestly. "I guess Erick's sword lessons have come in handy."

Ingolf winced. He remembered the number of times during the long winter months he had chided the young man for teaching a woman, a slave for that matter, the art of sword warfare with the wooden practice blades. As he limped over to help move the heavy prisoner, he raised his right hand.

"I promise never to tease young Erick about the lessons again."

Kiera grinned with pride.

Ingolf sat down heavily against the wall, where the women tended to the bleeding wound in his thigh. In a few minutes, they had the bleeding under control. They raised his injured leg off the ground with several folded blankets. It was then that Bjorn returned. He was there only for an instant, but the words he uttered sent a wave of relief throughout the longhouse.

"It's over."

*   *   *

Early the next morning, the entire village gathered around the charred mound that had once been the animal stable. Everyone murmured quietly, still trying to digest the events of the night. Thorfinn raised his hand to quiet them.

"The attack that occurred last night was a shock to us all. Our animal shelter is gone. One sheep will likely not survive due to the burns it has received. Another cow has been injured with a spear. We have also lost most of yesterday's salmon catch. The intruders threw the fish into the fire before we could stop them. As well, Ingolf and Bjarni were hurt. Thankfully, no one lost their life during the attack."

The crowd turned as the captured skraeling was led out of a house, still tied, and escorted by two of the biggest men of the village to the centre of the gathering. His face wore a stony, unrepentant expression. His dark, narrow eyes showed no emotion. The war markings on his face were smeared, but the wings of the eagle could still be clearly seen. Many cursed him as he walked passed, some threatening his life. They brought the captive to Thorfinn. Thorfinn stared at the intruder for a moment, then turned to face the villagers.

"We must also remember that what happened last night could have been much, much worse. No one lost their lives. They did not burn our ships. Although this man did burst in among our families, I'm not convinced that he was trying to hurt anyone. I have a suspicion that he was only trying to scare us."

"He did a good job of that!" exclaimed Dagmar. "You were not there, Thorfinn. I thought he was going to take that harpoon and ram it right through Ingrid! Who knows what he would have done had Kiera not stopped him."

Dagmar put an arm around Kiera. The skraeling's cold eyes turned and focused on her, as if he were memorizing the face of the woman who had brought him to this end. She shifted uncomfortably, trying not to imagine what he might be thinking as he looked at her. The angry crowd shouted out ideas for his punishment. Thorfinn held up his hand once again and waited for calm.

"We must remember, people, that although trained to defend ourselves, we came to Vinland looking for a peaceful home. There are less than fifty of us in our community. We have already seen well over a hundred skraeling fighters. The numbers, therefore, are not in our favour."

"But it's not fair," lamented Ingrid. "We didn't start this war!"

Thorfinn nodded. "That's true. On a different

expedition, our brother Thorwald started this war years ago. He had a bloody encounter with the skraelings, killing several of them before they killed him. If we are to survive in this land, then this cycle of violence must end. If we choose to harm him, we will be declaring a continued war against his people. It would be a war we will not win. We must offer them peace."

"What can we do?" shouted a villager.

"We can let him go," Thorfinn said simply.

Murmurs of disbelief swept through the crowd. Thorfinn quieted them.

"If we let him go, we can hope that our kindness to him will be a turning point in our relationship with his people. They may then allow us to remain in this very place and continue our new life in this beautiful land."

"What if he returns with an even larger number of warriors and attacks us again?" asked Dagmar. "What then? We may all be killed."

He nodded. "That, too, is a possibility. That is why we must also prepare for the worst. It is therefore essential that we put together an evacuation plan."

"Evacuation?" another woman shouted, "Do you mean leave? Again?"

Thorfinn's shoulders sagged slightly. "If it means our survival, then I'm afraid leaving may be our only option."

"But to where?" asked a third. "Back to Greenland? We were barely surviving there when we left it."

"That will be our last resort, Olga. We may have

another option. Tomorrow, we will begin preparation for a new scouting expedition to the south. Perhaps we can find a better place to start again beyond these shores of Vinland."

"So what do we do with him?" asked one of the guards, pointing his thumb at the prisoner.

Thorfinn walked up to the skraeling, grabbed his shoulders and pushed him down onto his knees. Then, taking a stick, he started to draw on the smooth dirt in front of him. Warily, the skraeling watched. Thorfinn drew two men trading items with each other. He drew smiles on their faces. Then, lowering himself onto his knees in front of the prisoner, he held up a delicate bronze necklace and placed it around the prisoner's neck.

"We are friends. We do not want to hurt you. Please do not attack us. Do you understand?"

Although the skraeling watched every move Thorfinn made, he gave no indication of understanding. Thorfinn nodded to Bjorn. Bjorn walked over to the grass and lifted up a small seal-skin craft that was completely enclosed, except for a small hole into which the paddler sat. A double-ended paddle stuck out through the open sitting area. Thorfinn stepped behind the prisoner, removed a dagger from his belt and cut the ropes binding his hands and legs. Thorfinn's wife passed him a small leather bag. The skraeling opened it and examined the contents. He seemed surprised to see dried fish and blueberries.

"For your journey home," Thorfinn said. He pointed to his kayak with an open palm. "Go."

The skraeling first looked at the kayak, then back to Thorfinn. Without a word or gesture, the man stepped over to the boat, placed the food bag inside the covered bow and climbed in. The whole village watched silently as the kayak and paddler disappeared around the bend of the river. Bjorn stepped up to Thorfinn and joined his gaze towards the ocean.

"Do you think it will work?"

Thorfinn looked over his shoulder and stared at the charred remains of the animal shelter. "We can only hope."

THREE

The following week was one of hard work and grim determination. The four longboats that had transported the Nordic community to Vinland sat dry near the river. Due to the bountiful and busy summer, it had been several months since they had last touched water. The raised ships were being sheltered under a crude, thatched roof for protection against both the drying summer sun and the ice of the upcoming winter. After a quick inspection, Thorfinn and the other men chose the smallest ship of the four. It was also the one that required the least amount of repair for what could end up being a lengthy and risky voyage. Originally, they had planned to do the repair work during the long winter months when there was little else to do. But last night's attack had changed everything.

First, they ripped away rotten planks from the ribbing and began the laborious task of repairing the damaged sections with fresh timber. Fatigue soon etched its mark onto the faces of the labourers as they ceaselessly sliced and shaped the plentiful trees into long, narrow planks. Upon hammering the planks into place, the mariners sealed the cracks in the hull with a foul-smelling mix of hot tar and animal hair.

From a small building near the sheltered ships, a bellows breathed a continuous roar, adding to the shipbuilding symphony of zips, bangs and curses. Bjarni the blacksmith, struggling with the pain of an arrow wound to his upper arm, ignored the sympathetic gestures of his friends and maintained a blistering pace of productivity. Kiera cringed as she passed the pile of soiled bandages growing outside the entrance to his shop. The burly blacksmith would simply change his bloodied dressing several times a day, while continuing to pound out the endless number of glowing nails and fittings that were essential for the ship's repairs.

The women, however, prepared for the upcoming voyage in a different way. Some were filling bags and caskets with food and drink. Kiera helped several of the older women mend the holes and rips within the worn white sail which would soon power the Viking vessel along the Atlantic shoreline. Her fingertips burned with pain from the endless number of self-inflicted needle pricks. She gritted her teeth and persevered through the discomfort, knowing that their future might depend on the next few days.

The women chattered continually to help them cope with the stress brought on by the attack. They never tired of matching up the single men and women of the village, debating the pros and cons of each couple, often embarrassing Kiera in the process, as she was one of the few remaining unclaimed young women. The possibility of marriage would certainly be a means of escape from her role as a slave. A marriage to a Viking would lift her to equal status among her Nordic captors. She wondered what it would be like to experience all of the rights and freedoms allowed to the Viking women.

Secretly, if it came down to it, she hoped that young Mats would be the first to approach Bjorn and Dagmar with the proposal of marriage. Mats had come to Vinland to escape the memories that continually haunted him. His young Icelandic wife had suffered a terrible death while in the grip of a debilitating illness. Kiera could tell from his empty gaze that even after all this time, he was still mourning his loss. But he had been more talkative of late, and the occasional look that he gave her from the corner of his eye allowed a glimmer of hope to flicker within her heart.

When bored with the talk of future couples, the women would then begin to reminisce about their faraway homelands. Kiera's occasional contribution to the conversations would often come to a sudden and painful end. Talk of home would instantly flood her mind with memories of emerald green fields and Celtic banter. Most disturbingly, the ghostly images of her parents, brothers and sisters would drift into her consciousness. The shadowy memories of their faces, the laughter and embraces, retained for so long in her young mind, were slowly being eroded by time. She was terrified that she would lose the memories of her family altogether. Her heart broke at the thought of the time that had passed since her abduction. Did her family still think about her with the same longing and grief that she felt? Would they even recognize her if she should miraculously make it back to Ireland?

Kiera was thankful when Bjarni stuck his head out of his darkened shop and bellowed her name. She politely excused herself from the group and trotted down the path to the blacksmith's shop. Sitting in a bucket of water, next to the bloodied rags, were two dozen blackened nails. She stuck her head inside the door, and heat smacked her across the face. She recognized Bjarni's silhouette against the glowing oven as his brawny arms pumped the hissing bellows. She noticed the damp, red stain on the cloth that was wrapped around his huge arm.

"Kiera, I need you to run these nails over to the ship. Mind yourself, though," the smith's voice boomed. "Those nails may still be hot!"

Kiera bent down and carefully touched the nails before grabbing them. Several were still warm. She scooped them out of the bucket and began the trek towards the ship. She smiled as she wandered through the colony of workers as they lovingly nurtured their thirty-five foot long, timber-lined queen. Kiera ducked underneath the arching keel and moved towards Mats, lying on his back, red-faced, and holding a plank up with one hand against the bottom of the hull.

"To the gods above," he moaned, "it's about time! Quick! Quick! Bring them here before my arm falls off!"

Kiera passed the nails to his free hand, then watched as he placed the majority of the nails on his chest, stuck the last two in his teeth, then, with three expert cracks of the hammer, drove his first nail deep into the plank. Slithering backwards, Mats worked his way along the length of the keel, driving in nail after nail, his hands flying with quickness and precision. Securing the board, he gave a great sigh, rolled onto his side and smiled at her.

"Thanks, Kiera. Sorry if I was grumpy a moment ago."

"That's all right," she said, trying to be casual. "How is it going with the ship?"

"She was in rough shape, but with all of us breaking our backs on this job, I think she will be ready to go in a day or two."

"And I guess you'll be going?"

Mats shrugged and turned his attention back to the hull. "Don't know. Thorfinn hasn't yet decided who's going, as far as I know."

She frowned as he began to repair another section. The short conversation was over.

"I had better get back to repairing the sail."

Only the hammer responded with a sharp crack. Kiera shrugged, turned and walked face-first into a sweaty chest.

"Better watch where you're going, young lady." Bjorn pulled her away from him by the shoulders and glanced over at Mats, raising his eyebrows. "Actually, I'm glad I bumped into you."

She smiled shyly, knowing that Bjorn wouldn't embarrass her in front of Mats, and brushed the hair from her eyes. "Do you need some help down here?'

Bjorn cleared his throat. "Not exactly. Thorfinn and I have decided that we would like you to come with us on the voyage."

Kiera's mouth dropped open. "Go with you? On the ship?"

"That's right."

"But I'm..."

"I know. You are a young woman, and it's unusual for women to go on voyages of exploration, but we really don't have much choice. We need every available man to stay behind and guard the village from possible attack. Thorfinn has decided to take only a skeleton crew with him on the journey south. If you come, then Gunnar, the only man who is skilled in sail repair, can remain and help guard the village. He can also continue to work on the other boats in case the village needs to evacuate on short notice."

Kiera shifted uneasily. Unlike many Vikings, she preferred to have dry land under her feet. "But there are other women in the village who are skilled at sail repair and life on the ocean than myself. Perhaps one of them should go in my place."

"I'm afraid that's out of the question," Bjorn said flatly.

His words cut her to the core. The other, more skilled women were blood Vikings. She was not. Even though Bjorn and Dagmar treated her as family, she was still a slave. Her life didn't matter. Clearly, her idea of Bjorn, Dagmar and Lorna being a second family to her was just a fantasy. If this is how her own family felt about her, then what about Mats? To the villagers, she was still an outsider and would remain so for the rest of her life. Her gaze drifted down to the ground to hide her watering eyes.

"When do we leave?" she asked, her voice hollow and defeated.

"Tomorrow, at first light."

She turned, shoulders sagging. "Then I had better go pack."

Kiera wasn't sure if Bjorn had picked up on her dejectedness. She wasn't even sure if he cared. Everything she believed of her place in this community was now shattered. She was heading out to sea, past uncharted lands and into unforeseen danger because she was expendable. She wiped her eyes and glanced towards the open ocean, looking northeast. Somewhere, beyond the horizon, was her home. She would soon be taken even further away from her soul. She stopped, reached out a hand and let the wind kiss and caress her fingers. Closing her eyes, she imagined her parents, their arms open on the distant Irish shore, magically sending the wind across the ocean to greet her.

"Please, mother, father," she whispered, "save me."

FOUR

The village gathered in the sombre stillness of the predawn twilight. The silence was shattered as the half-dozen ropes that extended across the river suddenly snapped tight, and the air was filled with grunts and shouts of encouragement. The boat reluctantly inched its way out of its comfortable home, sliding over the wet, grassy meadow and towards the waiting water. As the keel touched then slurped into the muddy embankment of the river, the ship gained speed. With a splash, the nose and hull gracefully slipped into the calm river. The villagers cheered. They pulled the ship alongside the village dock and extended a wide gangplank across to the midship's gunwale. The men and women formed a chain and began to load the mountain of packed provisions onto the ship.

The rising sun winked above the horizon, setting the majestic ocean ablaze with deep crimson. The men gave their loved ones a tender hug and said their goodbyes. Kiera stood quietly at the edge of the crowd, looking off into the distance. A hand came to rest on her shoulder. She turned and looked into the kind eyes of Dagmar. Lorna, still sleepy, clung to her mother's leg.

"We will miss you."

"And I you," she said, half-smiling.

"Please don't go," begged Lorna. She looked forlorn.

Kiera smiled, grabbed her under the arms and lifted her up. Lorna wrapped herself around Kiera's neck and buried her face in her auburn hair. Kiera gently stroked her head.

"Listen, Lorna, the village needs you. You will have to be a good helper to your mother while I'm away. And when I get back, I want you to show me your weaving. Finish the basket that we started before I return, and I will be very impressed."

Lorna nodded, her face still crestfallen.

"Are you well?" Dagmar asked. "You've been so quiet."

Kiera shrugged and looked down. "You know how I feel about boats. I'll be glad when we get back."

"Well, think of it as an adventure. The men certainly do. They haven't even set sail yet, and already they're singing sagas about the great deeds they think they will accomplish."

Keira sighed, looked up and tried to smile. "Thanks. I'll try."

"And you still have my needles?"

She patted her skirt. "Right here in the hem."

"Well," Dagmar stepped forward and embraced her. "Good luck."

Kiera held onto Dagmar, her heart aching, wishing she could feel towards her now what she had felt only a day earlier.

"I'll be back soon."

She gave Lorna a final kiss on the forehead. "Don't you grow up on me while I am away."

Lorna nodded, a tear trickling down her cheek.

"Kiera, let's go!"

Thorfinn was shouting from the stern of the boat. Already the men were on board and making the final preparations for departure. Kiera grabbed her sack of clothing and ran for the walkway. As soon as she had stepped over the side, the remaining men pulled the gangplank back to shore. The boat started to drift downriver. Thorfinn, manning the large, paddle-shaped rudder that was attached to the side of the stern, worked the boat towards the middle of the waterway.

Kiera moved to the front of the boat and took her seat, facing backwards, at the right front oar. Never in the villagers' memories had a woman ever been given the duty of rowing a longboat alongside Viking men, and from the looks that she was receiving from the eleven others, her adventure was about to start as soon as she touched the rough handle floating in front of her. Beside her, manning the opposite oar, sat Mats. She swallowed hard. The last thing she wanted was to look like a fool in front of him. She grabbed hold of the handle with both hands.

"Ready,men... Steady the oars. On my count...heave!"

The oars dipped into the water, and every set of arms hauled hard on the handles.

"Heave!"

Kiera could feel the ship accelerate as she grunted with each pull.

"Heave!"

Through the oar hole, she could see the riverbank zip by. She was amazed at the speed they had already achieved.

"Heave!"

They only rowed for a short while, but to Kiera, it felt like an entire day had already passed. Not used to such exertion, the muscles in her forearms had tightened into fiery knots. When Thorfinn finally told them to stow the oars, the command could not have come soon enough. Her arms shook, and she barely had the strength left to pull in the heavy piece of lumber and store it on the floor of the open hull.

"Prepare the sail!"

Kiera had been rehearsing her duties all the previous evening with several of the other sailors. For practice, they had rigged one of the other boats still in need of repair. Thorfinn had shown her how to tie the sail lines off to the wooden stays located on either side of the bow. She had to learn many new sailing terms such as starboard, port, come about, release, trim and hoist so that she could respond to Thorfinn's commands and become a seamless part of the crew. As the sail was hoisted up the length of the mast, Kiera took a deep breath and focused on the two ropes to the side of her.

"Haul in the starboard lines!"

Kiera quickly unwrapped the forward rope from the starboard stay. Using the stay as a pulley, she hauled in the rope as quickly as possible, trying her best to ignore her complaining arm muscles.

"Trim the bowline!" Thorfinn howled. She hauled in the second rope. "Again! Again! Good! Stave off the line and secure the portside."

Kiera's hands worked quickly, making both lines taut. The skin of her palms began to smoulder from the rough surface of the rope. She nearly lost her balance as the wind caught the sail, and the boat leapt ahead like a freed stallion. The crew shouted a whoop of joy. These were the descendents of the one of the greatest sailing nations ever to grace the open ocean. Ocean water ran in their veins. Kiera noticed the joy in their eyes as they shook their fists in the air and smacked each other on the back.

"A toast to a good voyage!" Thorfinn shouted.

Another whoop from the crew. Bjorn removed the cover of a cask filled with warm ale and lowered a large wooden stein into the liquid. The stein was passed to Thorfinn, who hoisted it up in salute to the gods, downed several large swallows, then passed it on to the next man. Eventually, the mug made its way to Mats, who had his pull, then handed it on to Kiera.

"Good work with the lines," he commented. "You keep working like that, and the rest of the boys will soon learn that you are as capable as any of them."

"Thanks, Mats," she said, smiling. She couldn't deny a certain tingle of excitement building within her. She let go of the anger and disappointment that had been eating within her all night. Perhaps this was to become a real adventure after all. She looked down into the mug.

"I've never had ale before."

He laughed and pointed to all of the casks in the stern. "Might as well get used to it. It's our main provision. Besides, I can guarantee it will help kill the pain you're feeling right now in your arms. Don't worry. Mine are aching too. Most of us haven't been out to sea in over a year."

She smiled at the kind words. She was thirsty. She brought the warm, brown liquid to her lips and downed several swallows before the thick ale in her throat and belly caused her to gag. She couldn't swallow and ended up spraying the remainder of the ale out of her mouth. Mats put up his hands too late, and his face received a shower of suds.

Kiera was horrified. "I'm so sorry!"

Instead of anger, Mats burst out laughing.

"You downed half of it before gagging. For a first-timer, that's an accomplishment!"

The rest of the crew had been watching the scene in the bow with amusement.

"Don't laugh too hard, Mats," quipped Bjorn. "I remember your first ale. You turned as green as seaweed and didn't eat for two days. I'd say she's faring a lot better than you!"

The second burst of laughter turned Mats' fair cheeks into a flame of red. Kiera didn't want to see him teased but couldn't help but join the merriment as well.

"If it's all right with Thorfinn, I think I'll stick with water for the rest of the trip."

"Of course," replied Thorfinn. "The lady gets whatever she wants. And you're doing an excellent job on those bow lines. Good work, Kiera!"

Thorfinn's eyes suddenly narrowed as he gazed at the sea ahead.

"Wind change! North, northwest! Prepare to come about. Release the starboard lines! Prepare portside!"

The jovial mood of the crowd evaporated with the commands. Kiera dumped the rest of the ale overboard, threw down the mug and grabbed the lines. Together the crew worked like a well-oiled machine, listening to the commands, guiding the boat onto her new course and continuing their coastline trek southward.

FIVE

After a night harboured in a sheltered, cedar-lined bay, the crew ate a breakfast of salted fish and raised the sail at the first light of dawn. Excitement was building, for by mid-afternoon Thorfinn predicted that they would be reaching the southwest corner of this enormous island and would start their more dangerous trek westward towards less explored territory. It had been over a decade since the westward lands had been explored by earlier Viking expeditions. There were stories of large native villages, huge tides, sea monsters, severe storms and ancient ruins. But balancing the dangers were tales of endless forests, plentiful game and delicious fruits. The crew was itchy with anticipation. If they could only find a piece of that western paradise for themselves...

Thorfinn remained focused on the task at hand; a safe voyage during a dangerous season. Being late summer, he knew from experience that there was a much greater chance of their craft running into an unpredictable and dangerous Atlantic storm. Although a Christian, Thorfinn continued to respect the ancient gods of his forefathers. Many Viking ships had been lost in such maelstroms, and his village could not afford a catastrophe. He could only hope that whoever truly controlled nature's wrath would look kindly upon their noble trek.

"We will stay as close to shore as possible until we must cross the open water to reach the western lands," Thorfinn explained. "It is there that I hope we can find a new, suitable home."

"The western lands," repeated Mats, in awe. He turned to Kiera. "I've always dreamed of exploring the lands of the sagas. Thorfinn is the only one in the village to have travelled with Leif on those early journeys."

Kiera tried to imagine such lands. "Do you think it's true? Are there really forests of fruits, endless seas of grapes and natives that live in villages even larger than our own?"

Mats frowned. "Of course it's true. The sagas contain our people's history. Why would we teach our children lies? What purpose would it serve? But, of course, sagas are a Viking tradition. You do not realize the importance of such tales."

His comment stung Kiera. Of course, she understood the importance of tradition, whether it be Viking or Celtic. Kiera had thought that Mats was kind-hearted and open-minded. Had she misjudged him so badly? She looked away in anger, but a hand rested upon her shoulder.

"There is nothing wrong with having a streak of doubt in your mind when you overhear an unbelievable tale, lass."

Thorfinn had moved to the bow and was now

standing between the two young adults. He had mistaken her anger for doubt of the truth of the sagas. "Your doubts are no different from the ones I had in Iceland when, over the roaring flames of the hearth, old warriors would tell the tale of the Ancients sailing across the Atlantic in leather boats only slightly larger than a barrel. It is said that those old Celtic mariners were already living in Iceland when my Viking ancestors first arrived in those northern lands. Being defenseless, they fled further west with each Viking advance, including Greenland. My favourite legend went on to describe how they had found the Promised Land, the one referred to in the Holy Bible. Some of the Ancients made the return home to Ireland to tell of their adventures but never to reveal the exact location of what the old Celtic maps had labelled their "Land of Promise".

"You didn't believe those tales, did you?" asked Mats.

Thorfinn laughed. "The combination of old men and ale often makes for storytelling that tends to, shall we say, stray away from the truth on occasion. But after living here, in Vinland, I now believe the ancient tales."

"Because of the Stone," added Kiera, smiling.

He nodded. "Aye, because of the Stone and several other stones that Leif and I found further ahead on the coast. They've been here. We believe they were carved over two hundred years ago."

Mats' mouth dropped open. "Two hundred years ago! That I don't believe."

"You'd better apologize to Kiera and her

ancestors right now. Those ancient Irish mariners are like ghosts. We have been chasing their movements ever since our people started sailing west. I tell you, what they lacked in ship construction, they made up in brains and guts."

Mats' eyebrows went up. "So there really are forests filled with delicious fruit and large native villages ahead?"

Thorfinn nodded and looked towards the shore. "Everything in the sagas describes the events of Leif's voyage. I have seen those forests and villages with my own eyes. This is a land of huge abundance. There is no limit to the amount of fish, game and fresh water contained here. We just need to find a place that will allow us to live together in peace with the native people."

"But is that possible?" Kiera asked. "From what I've seen, we are not exactly welcomed guests."

"It's true that the skraelings are everywhere, but some are different from others. The first Vikings to make contact with the skraelings to the north of our settlement had a misunderstanding which led to an argument. A fight broke out. Men on both sides were killed. The northern skraelings still remember that ill-fated moment. We think that it is why we are still attacked today.

"But Leif and I met other skraelings to the south who were friendly. That is where our hope lies. We are going to sail to the land of the Mi'kmaq. They were a friendly people and welcomed us as we resupplied our ship all those years ago. We will travel to their settlement and ask permission to build our own settlement in their lands."

Thorfinn paused, then looked carefully at the passing shoreline. "We are being watched." Mats and Kiera turned their heads towards the shore.

"Where?" they asked.

"Among that clump of cedars over there," he pointed. "Just above the rock face. Look for a dark red colour."

Kiera squinted in the afternoon sunlight and searched the shadows among the thick evergreens. What seemed like a dark red stone along the craggy shore suddenly shrank and disappeared.

"I saw it!" she shouted.

"Where?" complained Mats. "I didn't see anything."

"It's gone," she said, excitedly. "But he didn't look anything like the skraelings that attacked our village. His face was such a dark red."

Thorfinn nodded. "Aye, you saw him all right. This tribe stains their skin with some sort of red pigment. Can't tell for sure, however. I've never met one face to face. They're like ghosts. You catch a glimpse of one, but only for a second. Then they disappear. I've never met natives like them. Curious about us, but extremely shy."

Kiera pointed. "Look! There's another one!"

Another red face popped out of the shadows further ahead and to the side of a large outcrop of granite. The head didn't move, but Kiera could almost feel the eyes tracking the ship. Wait, not the ship. She swore that the eyes were tracking her! But before she could investigate further, the native vanished.

The game of "Spot the Skraeling" carried on for

the next half-hour. A face would suddenly appear among the bushes and rocks along the shore, and the crew would burst into a frenzied shouting match, debating who had spotted the red native first. The game helped to break the monotony of the day. A count had been started to see who had the keenest eyesight.

Using the rudder, Thorfinn turned the bow into the wind as he prepared to pass beyond the famous southwest point of the island. The game was ended as the crew adjusted the sails for the change in attack. Thorfinn smiled proudly as he watched them work as one. Given the short length of time he'd had to train the crew, it was a minor miracle that the voyage had progressed so smoothly.

Then, as the point drifted past and the south opened up into a wide vista of endless ocean, Thorfinn gasped in horror. His eyes were transfixed upon a distant black curtain of darkness that was sweeping the sea into a frenzied froth. The blistering edge of a darkened weather front was moving across the ocean at an incredible speed. The tempest was heading directly towards them.

"Lower the sail! Oars in the water! Mats! Kiera! Get that sail down now!"

Thorfinn glanced from the approaching storm front to the top of the sail that was slowly sliding in spurts down the mast. He timed the effort and looked back at the approaching curtain of death. It was going to be close. If the storm hit with the sail up, they would all be dead.

The bow was still pointing west, and the storm

was coming at them from the south. They had to move the bow directly into the storm or risk capsizing.

"Starboard oars! In the water! Pull for your life! Hurry!"

Kiera and Mats glanced at the approaching wall of cloud that threatened to destroy them. The wind began to whip and swirl around their legs. It was about to hit. They knew that the next few seconds would decide if they would live or die. They had to secure the sail.

They worked the ropes feverishly, lowering the top boom until the great square sail rested upon the lower boom. The bunched-up cloth was already starting to thrash frantically against their working hands. Mats and Kiera flung short ropes around the circumference of the sail and booms, lashing them together to prevent the wind from attacking the cloth.

The boat began to heave violently in the towering waves. Kiera lost her balance on the pitching deck as she and Mats tried to retreat to their seats.

"Well done!" shouted Thorfinn over the ominous thunder of the wind and waves. "Quickly! Tie off the sail lines, then brace yourselves! It's about to hit!"

Kiera quickly looped the rope around the stay next to her seat then hunkered down low against the railing.

The storm was upon them.

Now deep within the throat of the tempest, the wind screamed into the tiny vessel, tearing at every sailor on board the ship. An arcing tongue

43

of lightning licked across the sky. The tremendous crash of thunder that followed had Kiera thinking that the entire earth had just been shattered. Lifting her head, she was instantly blinded by a sudden crash of sea water. Everyone held on for their lives. The bow rocketed up the face of a tremendous wave, and for a moment, Kiera felt as weightless as a feather. Her body left the bench until suddenly, she crashed hard into the ribbing between the benches as the ship zoomed down the back side of the wave. As the bow shot up the face of the next swell, a loud crack caused her to glance over her shoulder.

A furious blast of wind had snapped one of the ropes holding together the lashed booms, allowing the wind to rip into the protected sail. The remaining ropes quickly burst apart, and with an explosive bang, the sail opened up its heart to the storm.

The world around Kiera slowed to a crawl. Through the rain, she could read the terror on Thorfinn's face as the sail flew open. She saw the gust snap the boom upwards. The crack of the stay next to her echoed in her ears as it broke away from the side of the ship. She could feel the sudden jerk on her leg as it was snapped upward, her ankle caught in the loose coil of rope that rocketed skywards with the wooden boom. She could see Bjorn's eyes grow wide with panic as her body launched from the floor, upside down, and soared into space. Her mind went numb as she realized she had been catapulted far beyond the safety of the ship. The ocean and ship spun like toys below her. For what seemed like an eternity, she floated within the storm, hoping that by some miracle, she would continue her upward climb to heaven rather than fall down into the gaping mouth of what lay below.

She fell. Face first, the ocean hit her body like a stone wall. The air was smacked out of her lungs, and she fell limp beneath the waves and into the eerie, serene darkness beneath. Only the sharp iciness of the water and her will to survive drove her arms into a drunken crawl for the surface. The seconds seemed like hours as the changing surface stayed terrifyingly beyond her panicked reach.

Finally, her head broke the surface, only to be lashed mercilessly by the salty foam of the storm. She managed to gulp in a lungful of air and sea spray. Gagging, she tried again. Her hip seared with pain. Twisting, she scanned her obscured surroundings. The boat was nowhere to be seen.

"Bjorn! Thorfinn! I'm over here!"

Only the howl of the storm answered her calls. She tried to clear the stinging salt water from her eyes. As a wave heaved her helplessly up into the sky, she waited, timing herself for the peak. Then as the wave reached the apex of its swell, she raised herself up and looked in all directions. There! She could see a dark, rocky outline to her right, just before the ocean sucked her back down into the trough of the next wave.

Moving her two arms and one good leg, she swam as best she could through the rough seas, waiting for each wave to lift her up in order to regain her bearings. The shore was not far, but the chilling cold of the North Atlantic had worked its way through her wool garments and was quickly draining her strength. She pushed herself onward, aware that each pull with her arms was weaker than the last. She was nearly there. The boom of the surf against the rocks was almost deafening. She briefly wondered whether she would make it to shore only to be crushed on the rocks. She had no choice. Her strength was almost gone, and death was not an option. She continued her laboured swim.

The next wave grabbed her body and threw her forward. She bodysurfed within the curl towards the jagged shoreline. The wave passed by, and what now lay ahead terrified her. Just in front of her were two huge, jagged boulders. A small gap between them led to the stony shore beyond. It was her only hope. She could feel the next wave building behind her. There would be only one chance. With several kicks, she lined herself up as best she could and allowed the wave to rocket her forward.

She almost made it. While her body flashed through the gap with the surging water, her injured left leg caught the sharp edge of the right-hand boulder, sending fiery pain throughout her entire body. In agony, she crumpled into a heap amid the frothing surf. Kiera was washed up like a piece of driftwood onto a rough beach of pebbles and rocks, tumbling until the water's momentum died, and she was left groaning in agony. Another wave swept over her. She writhed and screamed as her leg twisted in the surf. Her mind tried to rise above the anguish. Staying in the surf would be death. She tried to crawl but couldn't. The next wave burst through the rocks, submerged her and again twisted her injured leg into unbelievable explosions of pain.

The wave receded. Gasping for breath, she let her legs hang limply behind her as she dug her fingers into the slippery rocks and dragged herself, inch by inch, away from the churning water. How long it took, she had no idea, but somehow she pulled her body beyond the reach of the surf.

The pain was simply too much. Exhausted and curled up at the base of a rock face, she could no longer feel the icy rain pelting her body. She felt her mind slip away from the horror of reality and into the comfort of inner darkness. She welcomed the peace that was awaiting her in the world beyond. Her life here was over.

Then, before she completely submitted to unconsciousness, she felt something touch her. There was a slight tug on her neck, perhaps from her necklace. For a moment, she willed her burning eyes to open. In the dark twilight, she made out the outline of a face looking down at her. Where was she? The voice! The beautiful language of her birth tongue! Heaven! Only in heaven could it be possible. The voice of an angel had spoken to her. She allowed the darkness to envelop her once again. Before drifting away, Kiera let the glorious Celtic words sink into her memory.

SIX

I t was as if she were trying to swim up from the depths of the darkest ocean. Kiera floated through layers of grey thoughts and foggy memories. She remembered the time she had burned her hand on the hot kettle, and the fiery tears as her mother bathed her injury in a barrel of cool rain water. She tasted the salt on the fish her grandmother had always prepared before the family attended evening mass. She felt the icy cold rain that had pelted her shivering body as she was led away, sobbing, in the hold of the Viking ship after the invaders had sacked her home and village. Kiera wondered if she was living her life in reverse. Was this the process of life after death? She searched for a beacon to follow, a light to guide her to the afterworld.

Pain! Her cry of anguish cut ferociously through layers of confusion and opened a cruel portal back to reality. Somewhere deep within her mind, she was aware that she was being moved, and with each bump, an invisible knife sliced cleanly through her lower leg. Her senses began to return. The thundering of the ocean surf was now only a distant rumble. The scent of wet pine tingled within her nostrils.

With great effort, she forced her eyes open. Perhaps she was still dreaming, for there was darkness everywhere. No. There was a strange shadow hovering above her. It looked like the upside-down and backwards silhouette of a man. In her delirious state, she found the angle almost amusing. What was happening? Under her, she felt a soft cushion that bounced in a rhythmic pattern. Her fingertips reached down and touched soft pine needles. It was then that she realized that she was being dragged on a thick bough of pine.

Before she could completely piece together her thoughts, the improvised stretcher jolted upwards as it struck something large and unseen. The stranger grunted at the impact. The collision rocked her body onto her injured leg. Unbearable pain tore through her. It was simply too much agony to bear. Her ragged voice managed a hoarse whimper before her tortured thoughts disintegrated back into the comforting darkness of unconsciousness.

*　　*　　*

Kiera's nose twitched at the tickling sensation of smoke. She wondered why she couldn't hear the children playing in the longhouse or the women chattering as they began the morning meal preparations. A gentle breeze kissed her forehead as she struggled to open her eyes. Something was wrong. The air in the longhouse was always stale and stuffy.

Kiera squinted into the bright morning light.

She gasped at the unexpected sight. Next to her was a crackling fire. Several pieces of fish were skewered on sharp sticks and were roasting above the heat of the flames. Her body lay within a small, shallow ditch that encircled the fire.

Suddenly, the memories of the storm flooded back. The longboat. Her leg! Her hands reached along her body, checking for injury as her eyes continued to adjust to the morning sun. Her injured limb had been raised off the ground, supported underneath by several layers of folded fur. A large grey pelt covered her lower body, providing her with warmth against the cool morning air.

Kiera ran her hands under the cover and found that her injured left leg had been secured from her ankle to her knee by several thin but firm pieces of hewn tree limbs and securely bound together by many pieces of leather twine. Whoever had immobilized her leg seemed to know what they were doing.

From behind, a hand touched her shoulder. Kiera looked up, then screamed. Two concerned white eyes stared down at her from a female face stained blood red. The woman's exposed upper body, along with the knee-high leather skirt, were also stained a dark crimson. Her hideous skin colour looked like the hide of the devil himself.

The reddened woman, holding a large wooden bowl, also screamed. She flung the bowl high into the air, its contents spraying Kiera and the surrounding ground as it spiralled skywards. The woman turned and sprinted away, disappearing into the forest.

Kiera was alone again. It took several minutes

to regain her breath. Where was she? Who was that strange woman? Could she have been the one who had rescued her from the beach? If she was indeed her rescuer, then she had frightened away the person who had just saved her life.

Shivering, a thought passed through her mind. Perhaps they were going to kill her. In the past, other skraelings had not hesitated to kill. But why, then, would they have bothered to mend her leg?

Tears began to trickle down her pale cheeks. She was crippled and alone with frightening people she did not understand. What was to happen to her?

A twig snapped. She wiped her eyes with her arm and turned towards the sound. Appearing silently from the stand of cedars was a man, completely covered in the same red stain as the woman. He wore only leather breeches hanging loosely from his waist. Kiera dug her fingernails into the soft dirt, readying to drag her body away in retreat, if need be, from the skraeling.

But the man approached no further. Instead, he slowly stepped sideways towards a birch bark basin. He knelt, held his stained hands up and opened his palms towards her. He lowered his eyes, cupped his hands and then began to splash water onto his face. With a piece of leather and what looked like a gob of animal fat, he began to vigorously scrub his skin. After a minute, he paused and lifted his head. Kiera's mouth dropped open in astonishment. His cleaned skin was much fairer than the dark complexion of the northern skraelings. His skin was, well, almost European.

His handsome mouth was framed by high cheekbones. His dark, kind eyes crinkled slightly as his lips curled upwards in a friendly but cautious smile. Although he looked older than her, she could not guess his age. His skin was deeply etched as from a lifetime of wilderness survival, but his eyes sparkled with youthfulness.

Again, he held up his open hands.

"I no hurt."

It was the voice!

"I wasn't dreaming!" she spluttered. "It was you who saved me!" She then realized she was speaking the language of the Vikings. She switched over to a language she hadn't used in nine years.

"You rescued me!" she said in her Celtic mother tongue.

"Yes," he replied.

"How is it possible that you know the language of my ancestors?"

He shook his head. "Story long. You sleep two days. Tired. Hungry. Must eat."

The spoken words were choppy, and the skraeling seemed to struggle to find the right words, but his voice was one of the sweetest things she had ever heard. She stared at him in amazement. Was she dreaming all of this? This was impossible! How could she be speaking Celtic to a skraeling who was living an ocean away from her home?

He cautiously moved to the fire and lifted a stick of fish. Then he turned and called into the woods using a strange language. The woman whom Kiera had seen when she had first wakened reappeared with another wooden bowl. She approached, her eyes fixed suspiciously on Kiera. Kiera noticed that above her left eye was a pattern of three black triangles that together looked something like half a flower.

"Please," Kiera said, soothingly. "I'm sorry. I didn't mean to startle you."

The man spoke to Kiera. "She not know."

He turned and spoke to the woman. She seemed to relax slightly. She then examined Kiera as if she was the strangest creature she had ever seen. Carefully, she set the bowl of water by Kiera's side, then backed away.

The man pointed at the water, then passed her a cooked fish. He also passed a small birch dish filled with a selection of wild berries.

"Eat. Drink."

Kiera held the fish. Her stomach rumbled at the thought of sinking her teeth into some food, but she hesitated and watched her visitors. She observed the two strangers as they removed the fish from the stick, then pulled the meat from the bones with their fingers. His mouth full, the man gestured again for Kiera to join them. Kiera could no longer resist. She attacked the food ravenously. The fish was delicious. She then realized how long it must have been since she had had her last meal. The food also seemed to help clear her thoughts. She looked again at her wrapped leg. She tried to move it, but a sharp pain fired up through her body and took her breath away.

The man seemed startled by her action. "No move!" he commanded.

He said things that she did not understand. Kiera, confused and in pain, shook her head. The man looked around and found a twig. He pointed to his shin, then took the twig and bent it until it cracked, then pointed at her, trying to tell her that her leg was fractured. Kiera eased herself backwards and stared up into the speckled sky. This was what she had suspected.

She was helpless. She could not move, let alone get home. What was she going to do? She was now at the mercy of these strange skraelings. It took a minute for her to recover from the shock. Her thoughts quickly returned to the fact that the man knew Celtic. Perhaps this was a key to another way home! The skraelings were still sitting across from her, staring, eating their fish in silence.

"Tell me," she asked, "how is it that you know Celtic?"

He thought for a moment, then shook his head. An answer to such a complex question was too much to expect. Better to step back a bit. After all, she wasn't going anywhere. She pointed to herself and smiled. "Kiera. My name is Kiera."

He smiled and pointed to himself. "Chocan. She Sooleawaa. We Beothuck."

"Chocan. Sooleawaa. Thank you for saving my life."

Kiera bowed her head in respect. Chocan stood up, approached her and knelt down in the ditch beside her. He reached out and reverently lifted up the Celtic cross that hung around her neck. He rubbed the intricately carved grooves with his thumb and smiled.

"No. Thank you, Teacher."

SEVEN

Kiera lowered the needle, held up the fine leather garment and examined it in the glowing radiance of the fire. Sooleawaa circled around the fire and knelt next to Kiera, her eyes widening in admiration.

"It is beautiful," said Sooleawaa, feeling the delicate stitching. "I have never seen anything like it."

Kiera, Sooleawaa and Chocan had passed the last several weeks trying to learn each other's languages. It was Kiera's job to improve Chocan's mysterious knowledge of the Celtic tongue, while Sooleawaa had taken on the task of teaching Kiera the Beothuck language. Although Kiera could now understand most of Sooleawaa's phrases, she was having far more difficulty getting her voice to imitate the strange rhythms and sounds of the different tongue.

"Your skirt," corrected Kiera, in embarrassingly rough Beothuck. "It for you."

"For me?" stammered Sooleawaa, shocked.

Kiera passed it to her. "Yes. My thank you gift to you."

Sooleawaa looked to her, then turned in disbelief to Chocan, who sat to the right of the fire. He was using the fire to help illuminate the fishing spear he was carving from what was once a maple sapling. He put the stone and stick down and admired Kiera's handiwork. The flames danced across his glowing gaze.

"Are you going to try it on?"

Sooleawaa needed no further prodding. She stepped into the skirt and pulled it up over the thin, worn skirt she had worn every day since Kiera had arrived. The soft, brown material fit perfectly around her waist, curving down her hips to just above her knees. Kiera was relieved that she had sewn it perfectly. Sooleawaa turned back to Kiera, her eyes as round as the full moon peering through the trees above them. She tried to stammer a thank-you, but she was so excited, she simply hopped up and down three times, turned and sprinted into the darkness.

Chocan laughed. "I have never seen my sister so happy. Thank you, Kiera."

Kiera put the needle back into the hem of her own skirt. She grinned with a mix of satisfaction and relief. The giving of a gift brought back all of the memories of the last few weeks. Seeing her friends covered in red ochre seemed now just a natural extension of their warm personalities. She was overwhelmed with gratitude.

"It was the least that I could do. You saved my life, fed me and kept me company. I owe both of you much more than a simple leather skirt."

He nodded towards the trees. "She has gone to

show the villagers."

Kiera turned her gaze towards the woods as well. "When will I meet the people of your village?"

"Soon," laughed Chocan as he threw another log on the evening campfire. "They know you. They've seen you through the trees. My people, however, still fear you. You are a pale-skinned stranger. I tried to tell them that you are not a spirit to be feared. They're still not sure."

Kiera straightened. "I would love to meet them. Is there anything I could do to help them not be so afraid of me?" she asked.

Chocan thought for a moment. He then reached behind the stump on which he was perched and brought forward a stained leather bag. Kiera recognized it.

"Your staining powder," she whispered.

Chocan opened the sack, reached in and took out a handful of the clumpy mixture. He held it up to the fire. "This is ochre. Ochre is part of us, just as skin is part of us. It comes from Earth, our mother. It is also the blood of Beothuck ancestors. When we wear it, ancestors become part of us. Live with us. Ochre connects us to Earth and ancestors. It makes us one with all there is. You understand?"

Kiera sighed. Why couldn't she learn the Beothuck language as quickly as Chocan had improved his Celtic? He had come so far, and now he was helping her make sense of this new world. Just as the cross around her neck was her connection to her family back home, the ochre was the link to their Beothuck family. Her thoughts were broken by the stinging bite of a mosquito on her neck. She slapped at it, but it was too late. Her neck now itched as she scratched at the annoying bite.

Chocan smiled. "Also, mosquitoes hate ochre. No more bites."

"We never had these little creatures in Iceland." She scowled, then paused. "I'm ready to try the ochre, if it's all right with you."

Chocan shook his head. "Must wait. The first time, the mark of the band is very important for woman. The mark must be done by woman. We will wait for Sooleawaa."

Kiera thought about all of the rituals performed by Chocan and Sooleawaa that she had witnessed since being rescued. They always cut and prepared the fish or meat the same way, singing the same melodious chant that gave thanks to the animal for sacrificing its life for them. They always thanked and honored their ancestors and the Great Spirit before drifting off to sleep. They often talked to the trees, wind or animals with whom they shared their forest home. Kiera now realized that these people were actually connected to the forest in a spiritual sense. They were so different from the Vikings, and even her own family who chopped, tilled and planted the world into an environment that was suited only for human habitatation.

Sooleawaa returned from the darkness. She was still grinning from ear to ear.

"They had never seen anything like the skirt before. They think you know magic. They think you are a bird spirit, weaving this garment as you would a nest."

"Thank you," laughed Kiera, switching to Beothuck. "I am honoured. You think I am a spirit?"

Sooleawaa smiled. "Special, yes. Spirit, no. I saw you stitch the skirt with my own eyes. There was no magic in your fingers. My village, however, did not believe me. They do not understand this thing that you call a needle and this rock, iron, from which it is made. You must show them."

"Kiera can show them tomorrow," added Chocan.

"Tomorrow?" repeated Sooleawaa and Kiera, together.

"Our band will be leaving for the Meeting Place very soon. Kiera will have to be introduced to our family before then."

Kiera reached over and touched Sooleawaa's knee. "Please...put ochre on me?"

Confused, Sooleawaa looked from Kiera to Chocan.

He nodded. "It is time."

He passed over the bag. Sooleawaa knelt down in front of Kiera. She smiled warmly at her pale friend then began to hum softly, closing her eyes and allowing herself to drift off into a trance. Her lips quivered as she whispered a prayer of guidance. Stopping suddenly, Sooleawaa took several deep breaths then reopened her eyes. Her dark, caring eyes locked on to Kiera.

"This is the way of our people," Sooleawaa explained. "It will be your entry into womanhood. After placing the ochre on you, I will mark you with the sign of a woman. It is also the sign of our tribe, our family."

"Like this?" Kiera leaned forward and touched Sooleawaa's three triangles above her left eye.

Sooleawaa smiled. "Yes. I will mark you in the same way."

Sooleawaa again started humming a low, wavering tune that flowed softly, like a gentle summer breeze. It was a melody that Kiera found calming. Kiera closed her eyes as Sooleawaa's hands placed the cool, refreshing paste on her forehead. As her swirling movements moved onto her cheeks and down her neck, the melody was transformed into a poetic song. Kiera shivered with wonder as Sooleawaa wove a tale of marriage, motherhood and love.

Soon, Kiera's exposed body had been entirely lathered in the red stain. Sooleawaa took a cool, thin piece of charcoal from beside the fire and gently pressed it down just above Kiera's left eye. Kiera closed her eyes and allowed Sooleawaa to complete the transformation.

The humming stopped. With the silence, Kiera smiled and allowed her eyes to flicker open.

"How do I look?"

She gasped in surprise. In the faint, flickering light, it appeared that a circular gallery of both old and young spirits had descended upon their campsite. Their unblinking eyes stared at her, assessing her and her new stained look. Chocan materialized in front of the crowd. He opened his arms and, turning to Kiera, introduced the entire assembly.

"This, Kiera, is our band, our family," said

Chocan, proudly. "They heard the song of womanhood permeate the woods. They have come here to welcome you."

Kiera looked through the silent crowd for a friendly face, but the sea of blank expressions remained. This was a welcome? They certainly didn't have the outgoing friendliness of Chocan and Sooleawaa. Chocan turned to the gathering and spoke quickly in Beothuck. The apprehensive, trance-like state of the onlookers seemed to crack with Chocan's words. There were rumblings among the older crowd, their gazes examining the strange, injured young woman. The younger adults shifted nervously. Some of the children clutched their parents' legs.

Kiera swallowed hard and wished she could disappear. What were they thinking? Would they abandon her in fear? Would they reject her and send her away? Given the grumblings, would her new friends, Sooleawaa and Chocan, now turn their back on her if the band should decide to leave her behind?

Finally, the woman who seemed to be the most elderly of the entire band stepped gingerly forward. Others shifted uncomfortably, unsure of what was about to happen. She spoke slowly in Beothuck, as if for Kiera's benefit.

"Chocan says she speaks with the tongue of the Teachers. She also has been properly initiated in the rites of womanhood. Look, she has the mark of our band on her temple." She moved next to the young foreigner and gently touched Kiera's charcoal marking.

Kiera glanced shyly up into the wisest pair of eyes she had ever seen. The leader's face, deeply etched yet full of life, grinned at her in full approval. Kiera noticed the three triangles etched into the craggy skin above her left eye. The woman bent over and placed a bony hand on the side of her face.

"What is your name?"

"Kiera."

"Kiera, I am Nadie. I am the elder of the band."

Sooleawaa passed the bowl of red ochre to Nadie, who stirred the mixture with her finger, then brought the tip to the top of Kiera's forehead and traced the shape of a cross. She chanted a phrase too quickly for Kiera to understand, and the gathered crowd repeated the words.

She cupped Kiera's face in her hands. "Welcome, my child."

"Thank you," said Kiera, touched by her kindness.

Suddenly, the crowd began to whoop and cheer, shattering the silence of the still forest. Several of the men approached. They carefully lifted the startled Kiera up off the ground. For the first time since her arrival, Kiera left the clearing. The band weaved through the dark forest, shouting and dancing alongside their new family member.

They had travelled only a short distance when the darkness of the forest gave way to the shadowy outlines of fire-lit trees. The trees opened up into a broad clearing filled with over a dozen roaring fires encircled by piles of fur bedding. A shallow, gurgling river lined the far side of the camp. Jutting out from the edge of the water were several strange yet elegant craft made of what looked like the papery bark of a tree. The boats were pointed at both ends and had a sharp wave-like rise along their sides. They were quite different from the skin-covered crafts that the northern skraelings had used to attack her village. Next to the boats were small huts venting thick smoke from a central hole in their domed roof. The air was saturated with the aroma of smoked salmon.

The parade entered the central sitting area. Some of the men sat down at a row of hollowed-out logs that were covered with stretched animal hides. They began to pound out a beat on the drums, to which the rest of the band danced and swayed. Everyone was swept up in a whirlpool of motion around the central fire. Some bobbed and weaved quickly like squirrels, while others swooped with their arms like the mighty coastline raptors. The air became saturated with booming rhythms and animal noises. The men who carried her, also caught up in the pandemonium, gently bobbed her up and down to the rhythm as they moved around the fire. Kiera smiled as she watched Sooleawaa and Chocan become totally absorbed in the festivities. Sooleawaa floated around the fires, hooting like an owl while Chocan loped along gracefully, his mournful howls revealing the wolf within.

The celebration continued well into the morning hours. The dancing eventually transformed itself into a salmon feast. Sitting near the band elders, a place of honour she was told, Kiera ate with her new family members. Sooleawaa and Chocan sat on either side, translating the conversations that to Kiera seemed to be taking place at a blistering speed. The elders were impressed with Kiera's growing knowledge of their language, and every member made the effort to welcome her into the family.

The last person to welcome her, a little girl no more than seven years old, was different from the rest. She barely made eye contact, mumbling her welcome, then rushed back to her place at the far end of the gathering. Kiera turned to Sooleawaa.

"Who is she?"

Sooleawaa swallowed the rest of her salmon and looked towards the distant girl.

"Her name is Shawnadit. The spirits have not been kind to our little sparrow. Her father died in a battle with the Thule several years ago. Her mother was killed when she slipped over the edge of a cliff last winter. She has no brothers or sisters. We, the tribe, are now her family. Just as we would raise any child, she is looked after by the women of the band. Her mother's death, however, has greatly affected her. She and her mother were very close."

Kiera sighed, thinking of the young girl's heartache. "At least she is not alone," she whispered to herself.

As dawn approached, the revellers eventually gave in to their urge for sleep. Kiera reached forward and touched Sooleawaa's back. Sooleawaa was already slumbering beside the roaring campfire in front of her. She let her darkening thoughts drift upwards into the brightening sky. She thought again of that little girl, Shawnadit, who had suffered terrible losses, but still had an extended family to look after her. From Ireland, to Vinland and finally to the land of the Beothuck, Kiera was being pulled ever further away from her home and family. Although happy to have her life after almost losing it, she couldn't stop a growing sense of emptiness from weighing down upon her heart.

As she closed her eyes, she rubbed her cross between her thumb and finger. Home was now further away than ever.

EIGHT

The village had been completely disassembled by midday. Kiera watched in fascination as the large, shell-shaped huts called mamateeks simply fell gently to the ground with the removal of several key support poles. Other band members stored the canoes under low-lying lean-tos for winter. Most of the belongings had been previously packed in leather wrapping, and were now strapped to the top of an A-frame of long poles.

"Ready?" asked Chocan, concern in his voice.

Kiera nodded. "Ready as I'll ever be."

Kiera grimaced, anticipating the sharp pain that would come when Chocan pulled the ingenious seat. The contraption in which she sat was itself a wooden A-frame made of stripped branches and secured with leather sinew. Chocan pulled from inside the frame itself. He leaned into the leather harness that strained around his shoulders and waist. The sinews in his arms flexed as he brought the simple sled up to speed. Kiera, herself, sat backwards in a sling designed of soft seal skin that was securely attached to the inner frame. Both her legs were elevated and comfortable as they rested on a wide leather strap. Beyond her feet was one of the support branches that connected the two arms of the frame. She felt guilty being so comfortable as Chocan guided the contraption from the fire pit to the edge of the glistening river. They joined the other band members who had already gathered by the water.

Satisfied that everyone was now present, Nadie stepped carefully onto an elevated stump so all could see her. She raised her hands.

"This has been a good summer. The river once again supplied us with an abundance of fish. Our brave hunters have provided our band with leather, fur and meat for the winter months. We have also been joined by a descendant of the Teachers. We have much for which to be thankful! Praise the Great Spirit!"

"Praise the Great Spirit!" roared the band.

"I ask Chocan now to step forward and bless the ochre."

Chocan carefully lowered Kiera to the ground and stepped up to the stump, exchanging places with Nadie. He took a large sack from an elder and held it up for all to see. He closed his eyes.

"Great Spirit, we are thankful for your blessings. Your land feeds our children. Your sky gives us rain to drink. Your forests provide us with shelter. Now we ask that you bless this ochre and make it holy. Bless this, the blood of Mother Earth, so that your people may be safely led to the Meeting Place, and to our people!"

The crowd exploded. "Bless the blood!"

The crowd suddenly fell silent. All heads were

bowed in prayer. Kiera scanned the gathering. A memory began to nag at her. This all seemed so familiar. Yes, the Church! It was a ceremony from long ago in her memory. The image of the communions she had witnessed as a child. That was it! Chocan was using ochre instead of wine for the blessing. It was certainly similar, but also very different from what she could remember of the event.

Starting with the oldest, the blessed ochre mix was applied to the forehead of each band member in the sign of the cross. When it was Kiera's turn, Sooleawaa dragged her up to the front, and Chocan applied it to her forehead as well.

As Kiera was pulled away, she turned to her friend. "Sooleawaa, Chocan mentioned the Meeting Place. Where is it?"

Sooleawaa smiled. "You will meet the rest of our family. Wait, you will see. We must travel far inland. The Meeting Place is to the east, beyond those distant hills."

Kiera felt her heart sink. They would be leaving the coast and taking her further away from the sea. She sighed. There was nothing she could do. Her leg must heal first before she could hope to go anywhere.

As the gathering left the summer site in an orderly convoy, she wondered how her new friends would react when she informed them that she intended to return to the Viking settlement. Would they be angry? Would they even help her find her way back home? If they refused to let her go, then she would somehow have to make it back to the Viking village on her own.

* * *

The band followed the river away from the western shores of the great sea. Travelling backwards, Kiera could see the faint band of blue water kissing the distant horizon as they climbed higher into the hills. With each rise, the band seemed to thin until, on the third day, the ocean disappeared completely.

Kiera's heart plummeted. Her mind swirled with thoughts of her Viking village. She knew that with their failed mission to find new land, the village leaders would have no choice but to abandon Vinland and settle once again in either Greenland or Iceland. Returning east with the Vikings would mean that she would be moving closer to home. It would be one step closer to Ireland. She needed to get back to the village before they left Vinland. But how?

Sooleawaa and Chocan sensed Kiera's sombre mood, but they were too busy with their own responsibilities to talk. Chocan, of course, was busy hauling Kiera and his supplies along the increasingly rocky trail. Sooleawaa was directly in front of her, following the crowd. Her job was to herd the young children along at a pace that kept up with the adults ahead. She was one of a ring of young women who encircled and encouraged along almost every child of the band capable of walking.

Kiera would have found the sight of so many excited, swarming children amusing if she had been in a more familiar world. The guilt of not being able to help her adopted family with the journey only added to her inner anguish. Her dull eyes stared aimlessly at the young crowd until it fell on a face that seemed to mirror her own misery. It was the little girl whom Sooleawaa had introduced as Shawnadit.

The young child dragged her body along at the back of the young herd. Her eyes were fixed on the ground, just ahead of her feet, and her face held none of the excitement radiating from the rest of the children. It wasn't right for someone so young to be so sad. Kiera's heart went out to her.

The path took a downward turn as the band followed the trail into a valley. Kiera felt Chocan pick up speed as gravity assisted his descent. She turned in her chair. "Chocan, could I ask a favour?"

Chocan stopped. He turned, his face strained with effort and shiny with perspiration. He took a couple of breaths before answering. "Yes?"

She nodded towards the children. "It's Shawnadit."

He looked at the little girl. "She's not happy. We are not far from where her mother died."

"If it is not asking too much, do you think she could ride with me while we go down the hill?"

Chocan looked at the load on his frame, then to the path running downhill, and finally to Shawnadit who, along with the other children, was now passing them on the path. He sighed but nodded.

He placed Kiera gently on the ground, walked through the group of children, weaving in and out of the little bodies, until he caught up to Shawnadit. With a nod to Sooleawaa, he picked the young girl up in his arms and carried her over to Kiera.

"I have a very important job for you, little sparrow. Do you know our guest, Kiera?"

For the first time, Shawnadit's big, dark eyes glanced directly at Kiera. Her eyes widened in fear, then she quickly curled into Chocan and looked at the ground.

"You see, little sparrow, she is lonely. You know it is Beothuck custom to ensure that all guests are welcome in our band. That is why I'm putting you in charge of looking after our guest. You are in charge of cheering Kiera up. Can you do that for me?"

Shawnadit didn't answer. She just buried her head even further into Chocan's shoulder. Kiera reached up and took the girl from Chocan. Shawnadit didn't fight the exchange, but curled up quietly in Kiera's lap, her eyes shut tight.

Kiera tilted her head. "Hello, Shawnadit. Thank you for being with me."

Kiera and Shawnadit were lifted upwards as Chocan took his position within the frame. "Hold tight. We don't want to fall too far behind the others."

And with a lurch, they were off.

NINE

Near sunset on their fifth day of travel, the weary band of travellers relaxed at a campsite located in a notch between what looked like the humps of two enormous stone whales. Upon arriving, Shawnadit had jumped from Kiera's lap to run and join in with the other children. She had not said a word during the entire afternoon, but Kiera did get her giggling with some of her attempted Beothuck banter. Shaking his head, Chocan would translate Kiera's remarks back into Celtic, such as "I like Chocan's hair. It looks like a nesting fish in the snow." Kiera would join Shawnadit in the laughter. It was a good distraction for all of them.

Chocan rotated Kiera's sling so that she could see what lay ahead. Kiera took in the change in scenery. The land was considerably scrubbier than that of the mighty forests along the coast. Below, she could see a wide, rocky valley. A river slithered its way through the distant rocky hills. On the far bank of the river, an enormous barrier of felled trees extended in both directions as far as the eye could see.

On the near side of the river, Kiera could see

trails of smoke, dozens of small huts and canoes lining the river's edge. Many people streamed between the structures, busy in their various tasks. She guessed that there must be over a thousand people awaiting them in the valley below!

Sooleawaa brought her a piece of salted fish and berries for lunch. Chocan, exhausted, lay down and relaxed in the highland grass with his hands behind his head. Kiera nodded towards the large village.

"Is that the Meeting Place?"

Chocan opened his eyes momentarily. "Yes, we will be there tonight."

Kiera decided to let the weary man rest. She turned to Sooleawaa. "Is that a wall of trees on the other side of the river?"

Sooleawaa straightened with pride. "It was created by my ancestors long ago. We use it to bring the Great Herd to us. It stretches for over a ten-day walk in both directions."

Kiera shook her head in disbelief. "A ten-day walk? That's incredible! How could you make something so big?"

"We use trees that were knocked down by great storms. Sometimes, we can push them down, like this." She put one hand on top of the other.

Kiera was in awe. "Tell me, what did you mean by the Great Herd?"

"Caribou," answered Sooleawaa.

"Caribou?" asked Kiera, shrugging. She had never heard the word before.

"It is easier for me to draw one for you."

Sooleawaa took a stick and drew a magnificent

animal in the dirt between them, long-legged with strong shoulders and neck. From its thick, deer-like head stretched an impressive set of antlers, and she finished off the picture by drawing a person next to the caribou. Kiera was impressed with Sooleawaa's artwork but was shocked to see that a person's head only came up to the animal's shoulder. The beast must be huge!

"Caribou," repeated Kiera. "It looks something like the deer we had in my homeland, but this animal looks much larger and stronger. The biggest animal I have ever touched is a cow."

"Cow?" questioned Sooleawaa.

Chocan's voice interrupted the conversation. His face bore a smile, but his eyes remained closed.

"Ah, Kiera, surely a caribou is greater than that fierce animal that you call a cow. You have never seen a caribou? You will see caribou...many, many caribou...very soon."

*   *   *

It was just after midday when they entered the largest mass of humanity Kiera had ever seen. Her farming community in Ireland had numbered, at most, a hundred people. The Icelandic town in which she had briefly stayed before being auctioned off as a slave was large, but never had she seen so many faces all at once. Everyone was coated in the same red ochre, giving Kiera the feeling that she had entered a colony of red ants. It was then that she remembered she was now just as red as they were.

As the band entered, the entire village stopped its milling about and stared at the newcomers in stony silence. The sudden stillness was eerie and unnatural. The only sound Kiera could hear was the rumbling of the river and the footsteps of her band as they made their way toward the heart of the encampment. Then she noticed that the eyes of the crowd were focused on her.

"Why is everyone staring at me?" she asked Chocan as casually as she could.

Chocan didn't answer but continued to drag her further into the mass of icy stares. Kiera could feel the fingers of panic begin to tighten around her stomach. She wished she had Shawnadit on her lap for support, but the little girl was nowhere in sight.

From her backwards vantage point, Kiera stared in horror as the mass of red bodies closed in behind them, cutting off any chance of escape. Escape? She couldn't even walk. She was completely at their mercy. She closed her eyes and prayed for deliverance from the encroaching nightmare.

With a jerk, her sling came to a stop. Chocan moved in front of her and took her hands. "Stand," he said kindly.

"Are...are you sure?" Kiera felt further panic.

He nodded. Gently, he helped her to her feet. Her legs shook with the effort. She smiled as her leg took the weight without pain. He shuffled her around so that she faced the same direction as the other members of the band. In front of her was a massive, billowing column of smoke, rising heavenward into the crystal blue sky. Between the band and the bonfire stood a man who appeared to be even older than Nadie. His long, leather garment and belt were beautifully decorated with beads and carefully-drawn charcoal pictures of forest animals. His leggings were emblazoned with sharp-edged, geometric symbols.

He hobbled slowly towards the band. He stopped at Nadie, sharing an embrace and a few words. Nadie turned to face Kiera, and both pairs of elderly eyes gazed on her. The old man worked his way through the band until his face was only a hand's width away from hers. His dark eyes stared deeply into Kiera's frightened face.

"Is she the one?" the old man asked.

"Yes, my elder," answered Chocan. "She has come from the east. She speaks the language of the Teachers."

The old man nodded slowly. Then, to Kiera's surprise, he began to talk in Celtic. "Green eyes of the Teachers. So it is true... Do you understand my words? I know some of the language of the Teachers."

"Yes," answered Kiera, her voice shaking.

"Are you frightened of us?" he asked, kindly.

"A little," she whispered. "I have never seen so many people at one time. I come from a small village."

"Ah...a small village to the east."

"Yes."

"But you did not come to our land by your own free will. You were a captive of those who brought you here."

Kiera was surprised. How did he know? "Yes."

"What is your name?"

"Kiera."

"Ah, Kiera. I am Atchak, Grand Chief of the Beothuck people."

Kiera looked down respectfully. "Thank you for allowing me to join you at the Meeting Place."

"You will always be welcome here."

He put his hand under her chin, gently lifted up her face and studied her. He stared again into Kiera's green eyes and touched her strange, wavy hair.

"Yes, you are very much like the Teachers. Legend tells of how they came to escape capture as well. They came to us with knowledge of the Creator, the Great Spirit, and offered to help us build a new world of love and respect for the Great Spirit and Mother Earth. Although the original Teachers have long since passed on to the world above, their descendants, like Chocan, continue to spread their teachings to the people."

Kiera turned to Chocan. It was becoming clear that Chocan was also of Irish descent. He didn't seem to notice her incredulous stare and continued to focus upon Atchak. The chief cleared his throat. Embarrassed, Kiera turned back to the Grand Chief.

"Tell me about your captors, Kiera."

"The Vikings?" she asked, surprised by the question.

"Yes. We have only heard rumours of them. Over the past few years, we have seen their strange vessels sailing our waters. We also know they live on our land to the north. What are they like?"

Kiera took a deep breath, her courage returning. The Grand Chief of the Beothuck needed her help. She finally felt useful.

"The Vikings are a people who live by conquest. My homeland of Ireland, the home of the Teachers, was invaded by the Vikings many years ago. They took what they wanted and burned to the ground any villages that chose to resist their invasion. They are strong and fearless warriors. They also take captives, such as myself. I was removed from by home and forced to become a slave."

"Slave?" asked the chief. "I do not understand. What is this word?"

"Slaves are people who have to do what their master, their owner, tells them to do. They are like a captured animal, to be used and to be put to work without reward."

"Your family, are they too slaves?

Kiera felt the stab of sadness. "No. At least I don't think so."

"Then they are back in the Land of the Teachers?"

Kiera nodded, trying to check her emotions. "Yes. They are in Ireland."

Atchak paused, then changed the topic. "The Vikings on our lands, are they warriors?"

She shook her head. "Some were, at one time, but no longer. They are settlers. They came to your land to start a new life. But they will fight if they have to. An earlier Viking explorer killed a skraeling chief to the north and since then, the northern skraelings have been attacking them.

We have had to fight to protect our village."

Atchak looked to Chocan. "Skraelings?"

"I asked Kiera about them. She is talking about the Thule people."

Atchak turned back to Kiera, nodding slowly. "Ah, yes, we know the Thule well. We have also fought them for many years. They have come from the north seeking more land. We will not give up our home easily. We will fight any invader, be it Thule or Viking."

Chocan looked at Kiera. "But you said that the Vikings to the north are only settlers, that they only defend themselves when attacked."

Kiera frowned. "Yes. That is true. But if they are allowed to stay and flourish, more Viking settlers will follow. The Viking warriors will come as well, seeking fame and fortune. If given the chance, they will take your beautiful land by force. I have no doubt about that. The Vikings would love to have your forests and fish for themselves."

The Grand Chief frowned. Chocan walked to a natural platform of raised granite, stepped up and repeated everything Kiera had told them to the large assembly in their native tongue. A worried mumbling rippled through the crowd. She could sense fear among the people. She hated to be the deliverer of upsetting news, but the sooner the Beothuck knew of the Viking danger, the better they could prepare themselves for future encounters. She liked these people and also owed them her life. Perhaps this was one way she could repay their kindness to her. Chocan stepped down, and Atchak now stepped forward to the granite podium. Several men helped the frail man onto the platform. He held up his arms.

"Enough!" shouted Atchak. "What Kiera has said will be discussed in detail by the council of chiefs. Let us not forget why we are here. We are here to celebrate our nation. We are here to rejoice in the return of the Great Herd. We must not let this disturbing news take away from the joy of celebrating these wonderful gifts from the Great Spirit.

"Now, Kiera, you have been welcomed into your band through our traditional passage of womanhood. Now allow me to welcome you into our great nation. Walk to me."

Kiera shook her head. "I...I can't."

"Walk." He repeated. Atchak held out his hand.

Kiera turned to Chocan, frightened. He nodded and smiled. Taking a deep breath, she took her first step on the injured leg. Again, there was no pain. She took a second, then a third. She carefully, slowly limped her way to the rock, where she was helped up to its flat surface. Standing beside Atchak, she watched as he reached into his pocket and pulled out a pouch. He held it over her head.

"Cinders from the Great Fire! Life consumed and reduced to ash! But ash is only part of the Great Circle! From cinders come life. A new forest. A new beginning. From life comes love, family and birth." He sprinkled the ash onto her ochre-stained hair. "Great Spirit, we welcome Kiera as one of our own. May she live wisely in the Great Circle!"

A whoop of rejoicing burst forth from the crowd.

Rhythmic singing and stomping reverberated throughout the crowd as it began to spin around the granite stone like a slow-moving crimson whirlpool. Kiera was overwhelmed by the sight of so many humans dancing for her. Atchak placed a tender, bony hand on her shoulder.

"Welcome, Kiera. You are not only a member of Nadie's band, but you are now part of the entire Beothuck nation."

TEN

K iera felt like a bird being released from a cage. Her heart was flooded with an indescribable feeling of euphoria. Freedom! Chocan and the elders had checked the damaged bone in her lower leg. They all agreed that her leg was healing well, but they warned her not to do anything too strenuous until at least the next new moon. Kiera thanked everyone for their kindness. She silently vowed that she would somehow pay them back for their care.

During the next week, with her limited mobility, Kiera did her best to help the Beothuck in any way she could. She worked alongside the women of her band, preparing the huge dinners for what seemed like an endless parade of hungry mouths. She also made sure the cooking fires were properly stoked with fuel. During the rare quieter times, she would play with and help supervise the many children. They loved her strange but exciting games and stories. They would giggle at her mispronunciations of the Beothuck language and would limp teasingly around with her as she did her chores.

Little Shawnadit was never far from her side. After a day of shadowing, Shawnadit had finally broken her self-imposed silence. Kiera was amazed how a little girl could go from a mute to a torrent of talk so quickly. Together they shared their different worlds, keeping both of their minds far away from their mutual inner pain. It warmed Kiera's heart to see the little girl brighten with each passing day. As they took turns stirring the soup, Kiera lifted Shawnadit onto her lap.

"Have you seen the Great Herd, Shawnadit?"

The little girl's eyes went wide. "They are big and loud."

"I've never seen caribou before. I'm a little scared."

Shawnadit took her hand and squeezed it. "Don't be scared. I'll be here with you."

"You'll look after me? When the herd arrives, you'll hold my hand again like you're doing right now?" asked Kiera.

Shawnadit nodded.

"Thank you. You're a good friend."

Shawnadit smiled, pleased that she could be of help.

Kiera was glad to have the company of Shawnadit and the other children. Chocan had disappeared down the swirling river with several canoes full of men to do last-minute repairs on the herding fence. Sooleawaa was busy preparing the hiding places from which the Beothuck would launch their attack against the herd of caribou. Thankfully, Kiera was able to put aside her thoughts of Ireland and allow herself to be consumed by the focused energy of the

Beothuck nation. Tension and excitement radiated throughout the entire gathering. The Great Herd would soon be arriving.

*   *   *

Early the next morning, shouts of excitement snapped everyone awake from their restless sleep. Heads turned. Fingers were pointing northward. The most distant pillar of smoke, only a thin smear against the morning twilight, was different from the others. Instead of a constant thin stream of grey rising slowly skyward into the calm air, it was a series of grey puffs. As Kiera rubbed her eyes, stood up and joined everyone else's gaze towards the horizon, the second furthest stream of smoke changed as well to a pattern of puffs. Sooleawaa, now fully awake, grabbed her by the shoulders and shook her excitedly.

"The signal! They are coming! Praise the Great Spirit! Quick! We must hurry!"

Sooleawaa hauled Kiera up by the hand and literally dragged her through the excited crowd.

"So early in the morning!" Sooleawaa yelled over her shoulder. "Never before have they arrived at this time. We must be ready, or all will suffer!"

Kiera could see the near-panic in the faces of her adopted family members as they scampered about, grabbing weapons and stone knives. She limped along as fast as she was able.

Sooleawaa stopped in front of her band's collection of spears, stone blades and quivers of arrows. Men and women cut in front of them, running towards the river. The entire village was near pandemonium.

"You have said you are a good fighter." Sooleawaa pointed her finger down at the weapons. "Help us."

Kiera looked questioningly at the selection in front of her. "I don't suppose you have a good, solid broadsword hiding underneath all of those spears?"

Sooleawaa shot her a puzzled look. "Broadsword?" She reached down. "Here, take Chocan's bow and quiver."

Kiera shrugged. "What's a quiver?"

Sooleawaa passed her a birch bark quiver filled with ten arrows and a strung bow. She also grabbed a quiver and bow for herself.

Sooleawaa waved her arm forward. "Quickly! Follow me! We don't have much time."

Together they weaved through the panicked encampment and away from the river. They stopped at the edge of the forest.

"Do you see the big tree?"

Kiera looked at a massive cedar at the edge of the forest that pointed heavenward into the brightening sky. She nodded, wondering what the tree had to do with the approaching herd.

Sooleawaa explained. "Its trunk is the size of a caribou."

"It can't be true." Kiera stared at the massive girth of the tree. How big were these animals going to be?

Sooleawaa pointed to Kiera's bow. "Now practice. Hit the tree with an arrow."

"All right," said Kiera, removing an arrow from the quiver and holding it in her hand. "How do you throw it?"

Sooleawaa, shocked at first, giggled. "You don't throw it. You shoot it with your bow. Watch me."

Sooleawaa expertly loaded her bow with an arrow, pulled it back, aimed and let go. The arrow zipped through the crisp air. It hit the tree with a smack and stuck, firmly wedged in a knot that marked the exact centre of the trunk. She pointed her bow at Kiera. "Now you try."

Kiera fumbled with the arrow. As she tried to thread it onto the string, her fingers became tangled in the bowstring, which allowed the arrow to slip out of her hand. The stone arrowhead bounced off her big toe.

"Ow!" Kiera angrily hopped on the other foot, rubbing her toe. She looked at her friend in frustration. "What about a small wooden spear? You must at least have a spear somewhere around here."

Sooleawaa grinned. "Spear? No. An arrow is much better for a caribou."

Kiera rolled her eyes. "All right, then, no spears. How about a nice solid cooking pot? I've been known to knock out a vicious animal or two with one of those."

"I would very much enjoy seeing you attack a caribou with a cooking utensil," giggled Sooleawaa, "but I have promised the elders that I would keep you out of trouble. Please, try again."

Sooleawaa stepped behind Kiera to help her load the arrow onto the bow. She then showed

Kiera how to pull back the string with two fingers and demonstrated how to look down the shaft of the arrow to aim at the target. Finally, she explained how to compensate for the drop in the arrow by aiming it slightly above the target.

Kiera tried again. The first few arrows were launched successfully, but they sailed harmlessly wide of the target. With each shot, Sooleawaa had to run into the woods to locate the missing arrow. A good arrow and arrowhead, she explained, represented almost a week of labour.

On the eleventh shot, Kiera nicked the side of the tree. It was on the twentieth shot, however, that Kiera finally stuck one into the heart of the cedar. Both women whooped for joy. Four out of the next five shots then found their mark.

Sooleawaa looked over her shoulder towards the river. Five of the seven fires indicated the Great Herd had passed by. Only the nearest two had not yet seen it. The caribou were almost upon them.

"We must go now."

Kiera had been focusing so much on her archery that she hadn't noticed the growing silence behind her. As she surveyed the open flat towards the river, she was amazed to see that the entire village had virtually disappeared. All the hut-like mamateeks had been reduced to heaps that resembled jumbled driftwood. Some men were floating silently in their canoes, hidden from the approaching animals by the thick brush that framed the open gap in the far riverbank. Other men and women were hiding behind boulders and dead tree stumps, weapons at the ready, waiting. Sooleawaa led Kiera back towards the river, and they settled in behind a thick, toppled tree trunk.

Both women relaxed against the curved wall of wood. As Kiera tried to imagine a herd of huge beasts crossing the river, a disturbing thought suddenly flashed through her mind. Her stomach tightened in despair. Anxiously, she bent around the tree trunk and gazed across the open meadow. Sooleawaa grabbed her shoulder and pulled her back behind the tree.

"If the lead caribou sees just one person," Sooleawaa explained, "the whole herd will panic and do something unpredictable. We must not allow that."

"Where are the children?" asked Kiera.

"They are kept safe in the thick bushes just downstream of the meadow. Why?"

Kiera allowed her head to bang backwards against the log. "I was supposed to see Shawnadit before the herd arrived."

Sooleawaa smiled. "I'm glad to see that you two have become such good friends. Don't worry. She will be kept safe until after the herd passes. You can see her then."

Kiera nodded. There wasn't much she could do about it. She tried to focus on her hunting responsibilities. "So what happens now?"

"We wait until the great leaders of the herd cross the river and pass by. We do not hunt them. They are the strongest and wisest of the herd. If we kill them, the safety of the whole herd could be compromised. We hunt only the animals that follow the leaders. They are the oldest and weakest. By doing this, we strengthen the herd as well as acquire the meat we need for the winter months."

"But what..."

Kiera's voice drifted off as she heard a rumble, like that of an approaching thunder storm. She looked up, but the sky was still radiant blue. Loose dirt rattled off the old log and slid down her neck. She had heard stories of the earth shaking in places like Iceland, but she had never experienced the terror of an earthquake before. She grabbed hold of Sooleawaa, frightened.

Sooleawaa smiled. "They are almost here."

Kiera felt dizzy, her heart pounded, and she put her other hand up against the log for balance. She glanced down at her arrows. What could a little arrow do to animals that could shake the earth?

Then the unseen river exploded with a thundering crash. The air suddenly filled with inhuman moans and grunts, squeals and thumps. Kiera curled into an even tighter ball. It sounded as if the earth herself had opened up and begun to swallow the river whole.

Kiera cried out as the most magnificent animal she had ever seen leaped over their heads, its grey-tan body sailing gracefully overhead, eclipsing the entire morning sky. Thick hooves clacked in front of her on the rocky soil. Upon landing, its massive hind legs propelled it into a mighty gallop towards the safety of the nearby cedar forest. Kiera had never seen such a magnificent animal before. It looked something like the wild deer she had seen near the Viking settlement, but so much larger! And the antlers! The intricate, branching horns that adorned its head were simply magnificent!

Her thoughts were broken by a caribou galloping to the right of the log, then another one on the left. A second, then a third, came flying by in rapid fire. So many caribou poured over and around their hiding place that Kiera began to feel dizzy. She felt as if she were an insignificant pebble at the bottom of a frothing river of fur and hooves. The noise was absolutely deafening.

Kiera fought the hypnotizing effect of the herd, lifted her bow and looked to Sooleawaa. Sooleawaa shook her head. They waited for what seemed like an eternity. Kiera could only guess that a thousand animals had now passed them, all reaching the safety of the forest in the distance. The size of the herd was staggering. She had never imagined that animals could live in such huge numbers.

Suddenly, a new noise echoed throughout the landscape. High-pitched screams began to build above the echoes of thundering hooves. Sooleawaa looked to Kiera, and she needed to yell in order to be heard over the caribou.

"Kiera, when we rise, scream as loud as you can. Fire at the nearest animal. They are tired after the crossing. Remember to aim at the chest. Ready?"

Kiera nodded tersely.

Sooleawaa rose, bow in hand, and let loose a frightening scream. Kiera loaded her bow and followed her friend's lead. She started screaming, too, but not out of excitement, out of terror. The largest buck she had ever seen was galloping directly at her! It must have heard Kiera's scream, because just at the last second, it started to veer left. At the same time, a blur flew across Kiera's field of vision and embedded itself into the white triangle of fur that marked the glorious animal's chest. Kiera watched as the buck gave a snort of surprise and pain, then careened head over heels onto the rocky soil beside her. Another caribou, a doe, couldn't stop in time and slammed into the buck's tumbling body. Kiera could hear one of her legs snap from the impact, and together they came to a writhing halt. The rest of the herd continued to stream over and around them.

Kiera, in shock, was brought back to reality by Sooleawaa shaking her shoulder.

"Come on, Kiera!" she shouted above the chaotic confusion of Beothuck howls and the bellows of panicked caribou. "We do not have much time! Shoot!"

Kiera raised her bow and took aim at a large doe, one of a dozen in a wall of fur coming towards her. The doe's eyes were wide in exhaustion, her nose flaring for air. Kiera released the arrow. It sailed just over the doe's forehead and landed harmlessly in the river.

"Too far away," yelled Sooleawaa, felling a second caribou, which flopped to a halt in front of their stump. "Wait, then shoot! Try again!"

Kiera reloaded the bow and scanned for her next target. There were still so many rushing towards her. She wondered if she simply fired it at the right height, whether the arrow would hit something. Then she remembered Sooleawaa's words. She waited for what she thought would be a shot that couldn't miss. Out of the frenzied charge, a young male came straight at her. Kiera raised her bow and stared down the shaft of her arrow. The caribou saw the log. At full gallop, he raised his front hooves and put all of his power into his hind quarters. She released the arrow. The caribou launched himself skyward just as the arrow struck between his front legs. The caribou flew over Kiera's head at what seemed to her an impossibly slow speed. The caribou was so close that she fell backwards and watched the magnificent animal continue to sail over her head. With the world upside down, she witnessed the caribou come back to earth. Instead of a graceful landing, the front legs collapsed, and the animal fell onto its side, a cloud of dust billowing up from the collision with the ground.

Kiera lay stunned at the sight until Sooleawaa pulled her back up. "Keep going!"

Kiera shook herself and looked again towards the river. For the first time since the herd had arrived, she could see flecks of the greyish-blue river between the dozens of caribou still attempting to cross and catch up to their leaders.

Kiera spied something much smaller than a caribou moving near the water's edge. It took a couple of steps, then curled up like a ball. A moment later, it straightened itself and ventured forth a couple more steps. Kiera's heart stopped in recognition. It was Shawnadit. The little girl had her hands cupped over her mouth, trying to shout, but the stampeding caribou easily drowned out any attempt at communication. Kiera didn't need to hear the words. She knew Shawnadit was calling out her name.

"Sooleawaa! Look! Shawnadit! She's out there!"

Sooleawaa lowered her bow slightly and joined Kiera's gaze. "Great Spirit have mercy on her! She is right in the middle of the herd!"

"We have to help her!"

"No! If we leave this log, we will be killed!"

"I'm going!"

Sooleawaa grabbed her shoulder. "Don't! Shawnadit is right at the water's edge. That's the safest place for her to be! The tired animals are just leaving the water and not moving at full speed. They will go around her. With luck, she will be all right."

Kiera shrugged off Sooleawaa's hand. "It's my fault she's there. I'm going!"

"Kiera!"

Keeping low, Kiera broke free of Sooleawaa's grasp, swung around the log and moved forward. There were dozens of wounded or dead caribou lining the meadow between her and the river. She dove for cover behind the first one, just as a large doe jumped over her. The wind from its body rustled the top of Kiera's hair as the caribou passed overhead. Kiera half-crawled, half-ran, picking her way from carcass to carcass and avoiding the trampling hooves. Halfway to the river, there was a wide, unprotected stretch of grass and wild flowers. She looked to the river.

From this distance, she could see the tears glistening on Shawnadit's face as she searched for her friend. The herd, lumbering up and out of the frigid water, seemed to make an effort to pass on either side of the little girl. But how long would her luck last?

Kiera didn't want Shawnadit to see her and move away from the partial safety of the water. She waited until the young girl was looking downstream, then she jumped to her feet and bolted across the open, unprotected meadow. Her injured leg was now the last thing on her mind. She accelerated into a sprint.

She was halfway across the meadow when an old bull caribou, seeing this strange animal charging towards him, took it as a challenge. He snorted, flared his steaming nostrils, lowered his antlers and charged at Kiera.

Keeping her eye on Shawnadit, Kiera didn't see the danger until it was too late. The sight of a charging bull brought her to a sudden stop. She froze. Where could she go? The antlers were lowered. In a second, she would be dead. Suddenly, something whizzed by her ear. The object hit the old bull in the front shoulder, causing his front leg to buckle. The enraged animal fell forward and cartwheeled, careening out of control in front of Kiera.

With the enormous tumbling boulder of fur and antlers almost upon her, Kiera did the only thing she could do. She jumped. She had almost cleared the animal when a flailing hoof caught her ankle and sent her into an airborne somersault.

She managed a full rotation before landing hard on her heels and bottom. A second of shock passed before she realized that she was still alive. She rose to her knees and looked back over her shoulder. Sooleawaa, now a good distance away, waved at her with her bow from behind the log. She had saved Kiera's life again.

There was no time to think of that right now. Kiera shot back up onto her feet. Shawnadit turned away from the river and saw Kiera. Her eyes lit up, and she squealed with delight. A nearby female caribou with a young fawn, just finishing the crossing, heard the strange squeal. She abruptly turned, identified the small creature as a potential danger to her offspring and charged at the young girl. Shawnadit, seeing the angry doe, screamed. There was only one way for the little girl to run. She spun around and jumped feet first into the river. Shawnadit's little legs were no match for the speed of the mother caribou. The mother caught up to her in a flash. With her head lowered, she caught Shawnadit in her stubby antlers and launched her high up into the air.

Kiera stared in disbelief. She watched helplessly as the little girl flew through the air, landing well away from shore in the deepest part of the river. Kiera ran through the remaining caribou and downstream to the water's edge. She searched desperately for the young girl. The frothing, angry water revealed nothing. Dozens of canoes zigzagged across the river, pairs of hunters slaying the slowest of caribou with long spears. Kiera cupped her hands around her mouth in desperation.

"Help! There's a girl in the river! Somebody help me!"

The hunters were completely absorbed in the hunt. Kiera's plea went unnoticed. Without giving up hope, she chased the water downstream towards the growing rapids. While doing so, she stumbled on a pile of brush. She glanced down to realize that the branches were hiding a spare canoe. A paddle lay inside on the ribbing. She threw the branches aside, pointed the canoe away from shore and pushed off into the current.

ELEVEN

Chocan was closing in on an old buck. The cries and smells of the hunt brought alive all of the instincts of his ancestors. His blood pulsed in excitement. He was one with nature. Predator and prey. Death or survival. Today, life had been simplified into its most basic components.

His friend and hunting companion Huritt sat in the stern. He dug his paddle into the water to keep pace with the swimming animal. The caribou's eyes bulged in fear. Chocan lifted his spear and aimed for the side of the neck. He would try to make this as quick and painless as possible for the animal.

Something thwacked into the side of the canoe. Surprised, Chocan almost lost his balance, nearly joining the tired animal in the river. When he looked down, he saw an arrow embedded in the bark below his knee. They were under attack? At the Meeting Place? That was impossible! Instinctively, he lifted his spear in defense while he scanned the shore for danger.

He saw Sooleawaa, bow in hand, on the shore. Around one of her shoulders was a long coil of leather twine for securing a mamateek frame. She waved at him, then pointed downstream. Chocan turned. A canoe with a young woman was chasing something that bobbed in the water ahead of the craft. They were heading straight for the waterfall.

*   *   *

Kiera was relieved when she saw Shawnadit's head finally pop up from the water. Her little eyes showed shock, and her lips were blue with cold, but at least she was alive.

"Hold on, Shawnadit! I'm coming!"

She did her best to paddle the canoe up to the little girl. The current was picking up speed, and the bow now bounced on the increasingly larger rapids. She reached out to Shawnadit with the paddle. After several attempts, Shawnadit's numb hands grabbed onto the blade, and Kiera carefully pulled her to the side of the craft. She hoisted her arms over the side of the canoe and pinned them, preventing her from slipping back into the water. Shawnadit coughed up water through her chattering teeth.

"You...you came for me."

"Of course," replied Kiera, "but we are still in danger. I have to get you out of the water."

Kiera tried to lift her, and although she was not heavy, every time she tried to lift Shawnadit completely out of the water, the canoe leaned over and nearly tipped.

"Stay in the middle," suggested Shawnadit. "Balance the canoe."

Kiera shifted closer to the middle of the canoe. She heaved again. This time, Shawnadit's feet came clear of the water. She fell into Kiera's arms. Together, they managed a tired laugh.

"There," Kiera said soothingly, stroking Shawnadit's hair. "You're safe."

Shawnadit smiled and looked over Kiera's shoulder.

"Kiera, look!"

The river suddenly narrowed into a roaring chain of rapids and rocks. Without guidance, the canoe floated sideways in the water. Kiera reached desperately for the paddle. The canoe's pointed ends suddenly slammed hard into two large rocks, bringing the craft to a violent halt. A wall of white water crashed into the upstream side of the craft. Water shot skywards like a geyser. Kiera pushed against one of the rocks with the paddle, trying to free the stricken craft. A sickening snap echoed beneath them. A huge crack in the ribbing tore open, then, an instant later, the entire craft shattered in two. Kiera and Shawnadit tumbled backwards through the hole and into the raging torrent. Bits of canoe bobbed along beside them as they were sucked further down the rapids. They slammed into huge walls of white water, each time being pulled into the frothing throat of the wave. They managed to struggle back to the surface, coughing and spluttering, only to be sucked under again.

Kiera fought the growing sense of panic. She maintained a tight grip on the back of Shawnadit's leather garment, towing the child through the endless cascade of rapids. There was nothing she could do but hope that the rapids would end before they both drowned.

Chocan shuddered as he watched the canoe shatter in two. His canoe had been only a moment away from reaching them. As he watched the girls disappear into the rapids, he wasn't sure if there was anything he could now do to save them. The waterfall was rapidly approaching. He turned to Huritt.

"Paddle as hard as you can! We must catch up to them!"

Huritt nodded. If they went further, they might not be able to pull out of the rapids before plunging over the top of the waterfall.

Chocan said a prayer as their small craft shot down into the rapids.

The men expertly weaved their way around the protruding rocks and over the waves of water. Chocan used his position in the bow to guide the canoe towards the two bobbing girls. The growing roar ahead warned him that this was a suicide run rather than a rescue attempt. Kiera, however, was almost within range of his grasp.

Kiera felt Shawnadit go limp in her arms. It took all of her strength not to let go of the girl. She kicked and pulled with her final bursts of strength in order to keep Shawnadit's head above water, often sacrificing her own gasp of air in the process. She tried to kick again, but her legs didn't respond. She sank deeper into the darkness. This was the end. Poor Shawnadit. What the little girl had suffered in her short life simply wasn't fair. This was all her fault. She cradled Shawnadit in her arms. Death was again reaching up from its watery grave.

Chocan threw his upper body into the water where he had last seen them. He grabbed furiously for anything solid in the liquid maelstrom. There! His fingertips touched something soft. Lunging, he grabbed on to it and heaved. Kiera materialized from the froth. Miraculously, she was still holding on to Shawnadit!

"Kiera!"

No response. He slapped her face. With a violent shake, she gagged and spluttered.

"Kiera, hold onto the side of the canoe! I'll take Shawnadit! Kiera, you have to let go of her now, or else we'll all be killed!"

Kiera blinked up into the bright sun. She allowed her frozen arms to let go of Shawnadit, but she was too cold to hang on to the canoe. As Chocan grabbed for the girl, Kiera began to slide back into the water. In one swift motion, Chocan hauled the unconscious girl into the canoe. He then grabbed Kiera before she slipped back under the surface. Huritt reached forward and pulled Shawnadit to the back of the canoe to make room for Kiera.

"Your turn now," Chocan said and grunted as he took on the weight of the waterlogged young woman. He hauled her over the side and let her collapse into the bottom of the canoe. There wasn't time to do anything more for the new passengers. He jumped back into his seat and grabbed the paddle. In the distance, both he and Huritt saw the horizon of the river disappear into a mist of nothingness. The roar of the approaching waterfall was almost deafening. Together they dug their paddles into the water and pulled for their lives.

They veered hard to the left. Paddling at an angle to the current, they aimed the bow at a flat-topped outcrop of rock that jutted out into the raging river. The boat leapt towards the safety of the relatively calm whirlpool that had formed upstream of the natural breakwater. The rock seemed to take on a life of its own, reaching out towards them, encouraging them to reach the swirling waters within its protective harbour.

Seconds later, Chocan cursed. Even with their muscular shoulders burning from the effort, both men were now realizing that the angry river would win this race against time. The current was simply too fast and too strong. It seemed inevitable that they would be carried past the rock and towards the waterfall's foaming edge of death.

Suddenly a person burst forth from the forest. It was Sooleawaa! She raced along the shoreline and leaped up onto the flat surface of the protruding rock. Chocan plunged his paddle into the water once again. There was hope after all!

Chocan and Huritt heaved on the paddles with an even greater effort. They came within a canoe's length of the rock tip as the current ripped them past its salvation. Sooleawaa was standing as far out as she dared on the rock's slippery surface. She threw the coil of leather twine at the passing craft. The twine landed on top of Kiera, whose face was still ashen with shock. Chocan reached back and grabbed the twine. He quickly wrapped it around the wooden supports of his seat. Huritt dug in at the stern and spun the canoe around until it faced upstream.

As soon as Sooleawaa had thrown the rope, she quickly backed away from the water's edge. She had only a second to make a life-saving decision. She would not be strong enough to hold on to the canoe alone. Three steps away, a jagged spire of rock jutted out from the table-like surface of the outcrop. Sensing that she was staring at her only hope, she dove onto her chest and wrapped the twine around the protruding stone. The rope snapped viciously taut. She grunted as the twine rammed her knuckles into the rough surface of the rock. Wrapping the twine around one hand then the other, she hung on.

There was a tremendous jolt. Chocan fell backwards onto Kiera, knocking the wind out of the already battered, shivering girl.

"Sorry, Kiera," said Chocan, apologizing. "Huritt! Get up here! Now! Sooleawaa's not going to be able to pull us in all by herself!"

Chocan grabbed on just ahead of the knot and heaved. He grimaced as he pulled again, moving the canoe only slightly upstream. Huritt reached over Chocan's shoulder and grabbed on to the twine as well. Together, the two men pulled again. Hand over hand, ignoring the blinding spray of water, they slowly fought their way towards the rock.

The twine held. The canoe finally made its way to the edge of the outcrop. Chocan leaped out first, rolling onto the flat surface. He lay down on his stomach and held onto the gunnel of the canoe so Huritt could disembark. Huritt carefully lifted the passengers out of the canoe and into Sooleawaa's waiting arms. Finally, Huritt himself climbed out, allowing Sooleawaa to knot the twine around the rock, ensuring that the canoe would not float away. Chocan crawled to Shawnadit and checked her breathing. She was all right. The four rescuers joined the child and thankfully collapsed onto the wet, cold surface of the rock.

After catching his breath, Chocan leaned over and eyed Sooleawaa.

"Where did you come from?"

Sooleawaa was wrapping a piece of leather around her injured hands.

"I promised the elders that Kiera wouldn't get into any trouble. The fact that I saved my brother and his foolish friend in the process, well, the elders will just have to forgive me. It simply couldn't be helped."

Chocan laughed. "Sister, you never stop amazing me. Thank you."

She stood up and lifted Shawnadit into her arms, then paused to give her brother a flash of a smile.

"You can thank me later. I think we had better get these girls to a fire and warm them up."

TWELVE

The next day, after a good night's sleep and several bowls of caribou stew, Kiera felt as if she had returned to the land of the living. Then, over the objection of Chocan, who wanted her to rest, she helped the band to process their assigned quota of the caribou kill. In total, her band was allotted thirty-two animals.

The first step in preparing the caribou was to remove the skin. She was shown by the women of the band the technique of removing the caribou hide. After the chest was sliced open, Kiera used a sharp-edged stone to detach the skin from the underlying muscle. She worked her way down to the back legs, over the rump and then back up along the spine. Her goal was to remove as large a single piece as possible. Given the lack of sewing skill among the Beothuck, the bigger the piece of skin, the less work it would be to make a winter garment. After the removal of the skin, she passed it on to other band members, who then scraped it to remove any remaining flesh or fat from the inner surface.

The next step was tanning. Tanning was achieved

by rubbing the inside of the skin with the caribou's own brain. The brain mixture would ensure that the skin would toughen and not rot, thereby creating a garment that would last many seasons. When the tanning process was complete, the skin would then be tied and stretched on a drying frame.

After skinning her fifth caribou, Kiera stood up and stretched her aching arms. Absently looking over the busy crowd, she was surprised by the appearance of a strange man who had wandered into the gathering of her band. It was hard for Kiera to guess how old he was, for his skin was not only covered with ochre, but he was also blotched with a random pattern of cinders and ash. His long, dirty hair was braided and hardened into thin, crooked pieces that resembled the flailing roots of an upside down tree. The man approached a dead caribou. The workers stopped and reverently retreated from the animal. He knelt beside the animal and began a mournful chant. Kiera was able to determine that he was offering a prayer of thanks to the departed animal spirit. The man then removed some fur from the remaining skin. He tucked the tuft of hair into a small leather pouch and moved on to the next nearest animal. He didn't acknowledge the members of the band. It was as if they didn't even exist. His eyes saw only the slain animals lying around him.

Kiera was so engaged in watching the man with roots for hair that she jumped when a hand came to rest on her shoulder. She looked up at Chocan. He held a small piece of birch bark in his hand.

"This is a piece of birch bark from your canoe. I

found it below the falls. I thought you might like it to help you remember your adventures yesterday."

She took it and turned it over, staring absently at its rectangular shape.

"I'm not sure that it's an event I will want to remember. Was your canoe still in one piece?"

He nodded. "Huritt and I portaged the canoe back to the Meeting Place."

Kiera shivered as she remembered, then turned and looked at the man chanting to her band's last caribou.

"Who is he, Chocan?"

"He is the shaman. According to ancient customs, he has the ability to talk to the spirits of the animals. He is required to release the spirits from the dead caribou killed by humans. The spirits will then go out in search of the birth of another caribou. Once found, the spirit will dwell in the new body for the rest of its life."

Kiera looked puzzled and returned her stare to the shaman. He was now moving his hands in slow circles over the heart of the animal.

"I don't remember that story in church."

Chocan moved closer and lowered his voice. "It is not something that is approved of by myself, my sister or the other Teachers. It is difficult for the people to let go of the ancient ways."

"So your teachings are relatively new to the Beothuck?"

"Yes. The true message of the Great Spirit is quite new for these people. Although they welcome my teachings, they are also reluctant to give up the old ways. For instance, I know that after they bring their young child to me for blessing with the Water of Life, they quietly seek out the shaman and ask for his acceptance of their child by the spirits of the forest. The shaman is a very powerful and spiritual man among our people."

Kiera gazed at the shaman, now wandering on to examine the animals of the adjoining band. "Is he upset with your teachings?"

Chocan looked over to the shaman with a hint of sadness. "No. But he refuses to have a conversation with me, not that he is a talkative one to begin with. My guess is that he is simply being patient. I think he believes that in the long run, his teachings will outlast ours, that the Beothuck will eventually return to their traditional ways." Chocan paused and sighed. "And he may be right."

"You said that the teachings of the Great Spirit are relatively new. How long have the Teachers been with the Beothuck nation?"

"Atchak was the first."

"Atchak? The leader of the whole nation?"

He nodded. "He started teaching here when he was a young man. When my sister and I arrived five years ago, I was amazed at the work he had been able to accomplish among these people. I had hoped to follow in his footsteps and perhaps someday be a leader myself."

Kiera tilted her head in surprise. "Did you say arrived? You mean to tell me that you and Sooleawaa are not Beothuck?"

"Although our great-great-grandfather was of your homeland, the place you call Ireland, our blood is otherwise part of the Mi'kmaq nation."

Kiera was completely confused. "Did you say Mi'kmaq?"

"Yes," explained Chocan. "The Mi'kmaq people are from a land beyond the setting sun. It is a very dangerous crossing to our homeland, and it is attempted only on rare occasions."

"So the Teachers from Ireland didn't settle here with the Beothuck. They settled in the land of the Mi'kmaq. Is that what you are saying?"

"That is correct."

"So you are a stranger to these people as well."

Chocan smiled. "It felt just as strange to me as it did to you when, for the first time, I smeared red ochre over my entire body. But the ochre is such an integral part of their beliefs that without it, they would always consider me to be an outsider. And you do get used to it, even like it. Ochre is like a second skin to me now."

Kiera looked off into the distance. "It sounds like the Beothuck are going through almost the same spiritual conflict as my Viking masters."

"How so?" asked Chocan.

"The Vikings once believed in many different spirits, or gods, as well. There was a god for the sea, a god for thunder, a god for the dead, plus many others. But several generations ago, the message of the Teachers began to find a home within the hearts of some of the Vikings. Unlike here, where the people seem to be able to accept both beliefs, the Vikings have split themselves into two groups: those who believe in the One Great Spirit and those who hold onto the ancient faith of the many Norse gods."

Chocan looked off as he thought about this information.

"Thank you for sharing your news with me, Kiera. It is good to know that the word of the Teachers is spreading among other nations, as well. Sometimes, I feel that our efforts in sharing the Teachers' words are largely in vain. Even in the Mi'kmaq nation, the numbers of believers are dwindling, and after old Atchak passes on to the next world, I am not confident that I will be able to maintain the seeds of faith within the Beothuck people. You can already see how the people continue to revere the shaman. Given the uphill battle, sometimes I feel like I should just give up."

Kiera placed a comforting hand on his back. "But I don't think that is who you are, is it? I can't see you being the type of person to give up so easily. You certainly demonstrated patience when it came to me."

Chocan smiled. "You are right. I can't stop. My faith, my beliefs are a part of me. I will continue my work, do what I can and leave the rest up to powers of the Great Spirit."

The sky was darkening, and cold wind blew in from the northern hills. Kiera shivered. Chocan led her to the warmth of a nearby fire. Kiera looked around at the band members wrapping the fresh meat and cleaning up the few unwanted remains. Like the Vikings, the Beothuck didn't waste any part of the valuable carcass.

"So what happens now?"

"We will pack soon. It is time to move the band into the woods and prepare for winter. In fact, I need to return to the river and help store the canoes for next year."

Chocan stood up to leave, but Kiera grabbed hold of his hand. "Thanks again for rescuing me yesterday."

His rugged face glowed in the roaring flames as he smiled down at her. "You, Kiera, have also rescued me with your words of hope. I thank you as well."

Their hands slowly, hesitantly, slid apart. Chocan gave her one last flash of a smile, then disappeared into the growing darkness.

THIRTEEN

Kiera examined the pile of icy brown vegetation. "Do you think this will be enough?"

Chocan threw the last slab of frozen moss onto the sledge and wiped his forehead with the back of his mitten. He was sweating despite the frigid weather. He stomped to the front of the sledge and grabbed the guiding poles.

"Let's go back and see."

They left the dark cedar glade and walked silently through the glistening trees. Kiera's breath clouded the air and hung like an unfinished thought. She pulled her caribou cape across her chest as a winter breeze tried to worm its way through her layers. The cape had belonged to an older member of the band who had died just a winter ago.

The chatter of children could be heard before they arrived in the clearing that held their winter home. It was a brilliant location. The clearing was surrounded by a thick wall of evergreen forest that would protect their soon-to-be-constructed village from the worst of the bitter, winter winds. A small but deep creek gurgled along the edge of the clearing . It would provide the band with a source of drinking water. Near the centre of camp, several men were digging deep holes into the ground.

"What are they doing?" she asked.

"They are preparing the ground for the caribou meat. We will put the wrapped meat in the holes then cover the food with layers of dirt and rocks."

"Why bury it?" she asked.

"There is simply too much meat to smoke. The frozen ground will keep it fresh. Putting the meat in the middle of camp will also help keep the scavenging animals at bay."

They trudged around piles of wooden frames. Some sets were in the process of being erected. Kiera watched with fascination as the two tallest men in the village worked together, the oldest sitting on the shoulders of the younger. The man on top reached up, took hold of the longest vertical poles, and pulled them together into a set of graceful arches, where he lashed them into a tight hexagonal pattern with thick strips of leather. The mamateeks in the centre of the winter village were already complete. The sweet smell of cedar smoke trickled out through the top vents and drifted through the still air of the camp like an early morning fog.

Chocan and Kiera continued towards an unfinished mamateek. The upper half of the curved wooden frame stood naked against the bitter winter air, while the lower half was in various states of undress. Both children and adults scurried in and around the structure. Several children dragged large chunks of birch

113

bark to the structure while the adults skillfully placed the pieces in a puzzle-like pattern, ensuring that the curved surface of their home was both wind and rainproof. Huritt saw their approach, greeted them and examined their load.

"I think you have enough to finish the job."

"Good," groaned Chocan, stretching his back.

"And there wasn't much moss left in the clearing, either," added Kiera. "The pickings were getting a little thin."

Shawnadit popped out of the mamateek and ran into Kiera's arms. Kiera flipped her upside down and tickled her until she squealed with laughter. As Kiera returned her to the ground, an older boy asked Shawnadit to fetch more birch bark. Giving Kiera one last hug, she skipped off merrily into the woods.

Kiera, Chocan and Huritt unloaded the moss from the sledge and passed the pieces up to the waiting hands that reached out through the top of the unfinished frame. The moss was then carefully placed on top of the layer of birch bark. Kiera knew that the moss would be used to help insulate the mamateek from the cold winter winds. In many ways, the winter mamateeks were similar to the low, sod-covered Viking longhouses.

"I think I need a drink of water." Chocan's voice was rough and dry.

Kiera stretched her back. "I'll join you."

Chocan grabbed two birch containers and led Kiera to the stream. As he knelt down in the snow and scooped up the water, Kiera stared into the quickly moving creek and thought of its journey.

The stream would eventually join a river, which would lead to the coast and finally open itself up to the endless sea. The ocean. Even the gurgling laughter of the stream haunted her memories. There would be no better time. She had to tell him.

"Chocan?"

He looked up as he passed her a container of water.

"Yes?"

She stared at her reflection in the cup. "I have to go home."

"Home?"

She hesitated. "To Ireland. To my family."

He stared at her with his dark, penetrating eyes. "You are not happy here, with us?"

Kiera lowered her eyes in shame. How could she make him understand?

"Your family, your band, your people have welcomed me into their hearts. You and Sooleawaa have also saved my life several times. And for all of these things, I will always be truly grateful. But you need to understand, this is not my home. I need to go back."

There was an awkward moment of silence.

"How?" he asked.

She sighed. "Unless you know of another way across the ocean, I will need to get back to the Viking village."

His eyes widened in surprise. "Return to your captors? How will that help you get home? You will only be forced to return to your duties as a slave."

"They are my only way back, Chocan. They will

soon leave this land. They do not have the warriors or the weapons to fight off the raiding Thule. Thorfinn will lead his people back east to the land of the Vikings, perhaps Greenland or Iceland. Although I will still be a slave, at least I will be another step closer to Ireland."

Chocan turned away from her and looked off into the distance. "You truly believe that the Vikings will someday allow you to return home?"

"I know it's unlikely, perhaps impossible, but it is still my only glimmer of hope."

Silence.

"When must you be back?"

Kiera tried to clear her dry throat. Was he disappointed? Of course he was. The bond that they had built between them was strong and real. She was choosing a life of slavery over a life of freedom with his people. Even with the fur coverings, she felt cold and hollow. She hadn't thought that telling Chocan would be so difficult.

"I think they will be leaving some time in the spring. They will need to get back to Greenland or Iceland by mid summer if they are to prepare shelters for the following winter."

From his profile, Kiera could see Chocan frowning.

"Spring. It will be difficult. During the caribou hunt, I asked my fellow brothers from the north lands about your village. They have only heard about it through their Thule captives, the ones who have caused your masters so much trouble. The Thule have been a problem for us also. They have taken some of our northern lands by force.

116

A war council was convened at the Meeting Place in order to plan for the removal of the intruders. Atchak and the other elders have decided that we will attack the Thule in the summer. To get you home before the Vikings leave, you will have to make your journey before then. You will have to cross Thule-held territory."

Kiera shuddered, but she was able to maintain a strong voice. "I understand it might be dangerous."

Chocan nodded. "Dangerous, yes, but perhaps still possible."

"I understand the dangers. I will also do whatever it takes to trade for one of your canoes. If you would be kind enough to give me the directions back to the Vikings, I will leave at the earliest possible moment."

Chocan shook his head, still facing away. "You cannot do it alone."

"I have to try."

He turned and faced her. "I will take you."

"Chocan, you can't! You are a Teacher. You are needed by the band, by this whole nation! I can't ask you to do this."

He stepped forward and put his hands on her shoulders. "I want to do this."

She tried to hold back the tears. "Are you sure?"

Chocan smiled. "We will have to wait for winter to pass, but yes, if it is your wish, then I will take you not to your home, but back to your Viking masters. There is a difference, you know."

She embraced him warmly. "Yes, I know. And thank you."

FOURTEEN

The winter had been long and difficult. Even though it was one of the most bitter in recent memory, the temperature inside the mamateek stayed relatively pleasant. Kiera admired the efficient design of the structures. Fourteen people lived within her mamateek, sharing both the heat of the central fire and the resulting smoky air. Above their heads, worn but colourfully decorated caribou skins lined the walls. The painted images of forest animals on the skins danced in the light of the crackling fire.

To pass the time away during the dark evenings, most of the adults and children enjoyed playing a game called Chance. It involved throwing a handful of beautifully decorated two-sided bones onto the dirt floor. The pattern was different on each side of the bone. The goal was to predict which sides would land facing up, and points were given depending on how the pieces fell.

Kiera also enjoyed playing the game, but she preferred to spend most of her spare time in a different way. She sat quietly in her back corner with Shawnadit, teaching her how to work the needle in and out of the small, discarded scraps of leather she had scrounged from the remains of the great hunt. Together, they sized and cut, sewed and hemmed, embroidered and dyed the small, leather pieces. Kiera was impressed with how quickly Shawnadit was able to learn the skill of sewing.

Occasionally, the other clan members would crawl over to stare in awe at their evolving creation. They were fascinated with Kiera's artistry and quietly watched her expert hands work the leather. Although everyone in the mamateek chattered in excitement as the garment neared completion, Kiera had made everyone swear to keep her project a secret once they stepped through the covered door of the mamateek and joined the outside world.

Shawnadit was seemingly attached to Kiera's hip. She mimicked Kiera with every movement and every gesture, right down to her harsh, choppy way of speaking the Beothuck tongue. Although Kiera occasionally tired of her shadow, she never openly demonstrated frustration towards her adopted little sister. When Kiera needed a break, she would don a pair of snowshoes and trudge out into the serene forest for an invigorating walk. In the stillness of the woods, she could close her eyes and let the icy fingers of the winter wind carry her home.

When tired of sewing, Kiera enjoyed spinning fantastic tales of her faraway homeland for the enthralled band members. She would also add a Bible story or two as she remembered them from her talks with the friendly priest in her village. The band members, however, were more interested in the mythical creatures and gods of the Viking sagas. They would beg to hear of the mighty battles of Odin and Thor against the various evil serpents and leviathans that lurked deep within the waters of the ocean. The Beothuk were as connected to the sea as the Vikings. Kiera's new friends also depended upon the salmon run and the plentiful birds' eggs found on the nearby coastal islands. The prosperity of both cultures rose and fell on the whims of the mighty water that connected their two lands.

After listening rapturously to the Viking tales, the elders would then in turn share their stories and beliefs of the Beothuck world. Kiera marvelled at the rich, detailed tales of life, death, war and the activities of the spirit world. Chocan would also spin his stories of the Great Creator. Sometimes they were as new to her as they were to the youngest of the band members, but occasionally, Kiera would recognize the story from her childhood memories. Kiera was amazed at some of the similarities, especially considering the fact that the original Teachers had first shared them with Chocan's ancestors over two hundred years before.

It was during a howling late winter snowstorm that Chocan sat cross-legged in front of the fire, his eyes aglow in the crackling flames, words fluttering from his lips like a distant dream.

"A man named A'kmaran lived in a village in a faraway land. He was comfortable there, with a large family and plenty of good hunting. But his family and the other villagers believed in many different spirits and feared many superstitions. One night, the Great Creator came to A'kmaran in a dream.

"He said, "A'kmaran, I am Gitche Manitou, the Great Spirit, the Creator of all things and the Giver of Life. There is no other but Me. Do not believe the tales of these people. You and your wife must leave your home and journey a great distance by canoe to a place of fresh water and good hunting. You will call this place the Promised Land. Once there, you will settle with your wife and worship only me. Your descendants will become powerful, and they will spread my word throughout the world."

Chocan paused, then looked around at the children. "Do you think A'kmaran wanted to leave his family and friends?"

"No," said the children in unison.

"Do you think he might have been scared to begin a long voyage to a place that he had never seen except in his dreams?"

"Yes," they answered.

"I think he was scared, too. But do you know what allowed him to begin the journey? He had faith. He had faith that the Great Creator would be with him, even though his friends and family told him that he was crazy for wanting to leave such a comfortable life."

"I think he was also brave," added an older boy.

Chocan smiled. "Yes, he was that as well. Without ever looking back, he and his wife left their village and set out across the waters in search of the Promised Land."

"Did he ever find it?" asked a young girl.

Chocan nodded. "Yes, he did. He was, however, very old when he finally arrived. But the Creator kept his promise and made his children and their children and all of their descendants strong and prosperous. So strong were the Creator's words that his story has reached us after the passage of a thousand moons and the distance of an entire ocean. The Teachers wanted everyone here to know the story. Two hundred years ago, they travelled all of the way from Kiera's homeland to ours in order to bring this story to us."

He turned to Kiera. "Do you know of this story?"

She nodded. "It is one of the Bible's oldest stories. In my language, the names of the travellers were Abraham and Sarah."

"Abraham and Sarah," Chocan repeated, slowly. "I will remember that. Now if you will excuse us, children, I must speak to Kiera outside."

The children moaned their objections as the two stepped out of the tent. They were immediately assaulted by the crisp, blowing winter air. A fresh blanket of snow covered the clearing and mamateeks, giving the conical structures the appearance of a group of smouldering ice-capped volcanoes. With the strengthening sun, the snow had softened considerably, allowing the two to stand on its packed surface without sinking. She folded her arms against the cold and turned to him.

"You picked that story on purpose."

He looked at her innocently. "Why do you say that?"

"You are subtly trying to tell me that I am already in the Promised Land. You told me yourself that the Teachers called this land Hyranason, 'The New Eden'. Just like Abraham and Sarah, I have made the journey across the Great Water, and now you are saying that I should be happy to stay here."

He shook his head. "It's true that I chose that story for a reason, but not for the reason you think."

"All right," she said. "Explain."

"You are correct in saying that you have found a sanctuary. We are your friends...your family. I feel the chance of you making it back home, assuming your family is still alive and well, is very poor, if not impossible. But you, like Abraham, are listening to your heart and the message the Great Spirit has placed within it. You will follow that message of faith, even though to everyone else it seems like you are embarking on a hopeless quest."

"Hopeless? Chocan, if this was supposed to be a encouraging speech, then you've failed miserably."

Kiera's face dropped, she turned away from him, closing her eyes and breathing in a deep lungful of biting air. Chocan stepped up to her and lifted her chin. Her eyes rose to his.

"Stay with us."

Her eyes filled with tears as she tapped her chest. "My heart, as you said, is telling me to go back. I'm being called back. It is something I cannot ignore. I could not live in peace here with my heart, when the Creator is calling me back to my family and people. I'm so sorry, Chocan. A part of me desperately wants to stay here with you and the rest of the band, but I simply can't."

He nodded thoughtfully, then looked up to the brightening sky. "Then we will go. We leave tomorrow."

Her mouth dropped. "Tomorrow?"

"If we are to arrive at your Viking village in the spring, then we must leave now."

"Chocan, I've thought about this all winter. You can't go! These people need you. I'll get back to the village by myself. Just tell me what to do, where to go, and I'll make it on my own."

She was interrupted as Chocan waved to Sooleawaa, who was returning from the creek with a large sack of water. She smiled as she approached, then noticed Kiera wiping away a tear.

"Kiera, what's wrong?"

"I don't know whether to be happy or angry with the two of you," sniffed Kiera. "What are you doing, letting your brother accompany me on such a dangerous trip?"

"Dangerous trip?" she repeated, staring at her sibling.

Kiera wrapped her arms around Sooleawaa. "I am so confused. A part of me can't stand the thought of never seeing you again. But deep inside, I know I have to try and get home, back to my family."

"So, you have decided to go back to the Viking village?"

Kiera nodded and wiped away another tear.

Sooleawaa brushed the hair from Kiera's face. "You must follow your heart, Kiera, or else you will always be left wondering about what could have been. And I do want Chocan to take you back. If anyone can return you to your village, it will be my big brother. He has travelled in the open ocean more than almost any other Beothuck. I, too, am your friend. If bringing you to your masters will make you happy, then that is what Chocan must do."

Kiera grabbed Sooleawaa again and embraced her. "Thank you."

Sooleawaa began to cry as well. "I will miss you." She looked to Chocan. "When are you leaving?"

"Tomorrow."

Surprised, she nodded, then broke into a smile that beamed with sisterly love. She grabbed Kiera's hand.

"Come, let's pack."

FIFTEEN

The entire village gathered at the edge of camp to see them off. It took all of Kiera's strength to fight the tears that once again fought to be released. All of the now familiar, caring faces of the band smiled or nodded to her. Quietly, the group parted, allowing Nadie to approach. Her ancient eyes seemed to sparkle as they gazed upon Kiera. She reached out and took Kiera's hands inside her own weathered palms.

Kiera choked as she spoke. "Thank you, Nadie, for everything, for saving my life, for teaching me so much, but most of all, for accepting me into your family. I hope you don't feel that I'm deserting you."

Nadie squeezed her hands. "We are only happy that your path brought you to us, if only for a short time. You are a special child. You have seen so much already and, I feel, you have so much more yet to see. Your path leaves us now, but who knows? It may be the Creator's wish to bring us back together once more. Either way, remember that we are always here for you and we, especially the children, will always remember you. You will become part of our family's story, our family's song. Listen for us singing to you in your dreams."

Kiera stepped forward and wrapped her arms around Nadie's frail body. "I will. Thank you."

Kiera stepped back, bent down and picked up her belongings.

"I have something that Shawnadit and I made for you and your family. Hopefully, when you look at it, it will remind you of my time with you. Shawnadit, do you want to go and get it for me?"

The little girl squeezed through the crowd, disappeared into the mamateek, and quickly returned. A smile spread across her face as she passed the folded garment to Kiera. Kiera unfolded it and held it up high for all to see. The villagers gasped, except those who resided with her in her mamateek, who smiled with pride. The garment was a beautiful, sleeved and hooded cape. It was fully embroidered around the neck and bottom with a pattern that mirrored the rounded mountains of the Meeting Place. All eyes, however, were drawn to the top and left where an intricate, geometric cross, made of triangles, diamonds and curves, had been sewn. The geometric designs beautifully built upon the sign of the band. The back of the garment was just as breathtaking. With artistic skill, a majestic caribou was caught in full flight leaping over a log. Behind the log, the top of two heads and two arrows could just be seen. Keira wrapped the garment around Nadie's shoulders.

"I made this for you and your...my family. The cross over your heart," she said, pointing, "is a cross from my homeland. It would have been the same cross that the Teachers would have known before they sailed from Ireland. I have always loved the Celtic cross. And if you look closely, you can see I began the pattern with the design of your band. Two worlds in one design. I hope you like it."

"It is a truly wonderful gift," said Nadie, holding her arms out wide and turning slowly around for all to see. "We will always treasure it."

Kiera now turned her attention to Shawnadit. "Do you have it in a safe place?"

She nodded and patted her skirt. "In the hem. Just like you."

"Good girl. You are very talented at sewing, Shawnadit. Keep practicing, and you will soon be sewing your own Celtic crosses."

Shawnadit stared up with her big eyes. "Kiera?"

"Yes, sweetheart?"

"When you are back home and you sew something, will you think of me?"

Kiera felt a lump form in her throat. "Of course, I will. But only if you do the same. Agreed?"

Shawnadit nodded, and sniffing loudly, wrapped her tiny arms around Kiera's neck. After a few moments, Chocan touched Kiera gently on the shoulder.

"Time to go."

Kiera kissed Shawnadit on the forehead and stood up. Chocan helped Kiera wrap the leather straps of her sled around her waist and shoulders. They tied snowshoes to their boots and fixed their outer garments until they were both comfortable. Sooleawaa wrapped her arms around them both and wished them luck. Finally, after many goodbyes and more tears, the two trudged off to the edge of the winter camp, took one last look back at their friends, and disappeared into the forest.

Although Kiera's leg had healed well, she found the going difficult. The forest was quite dense along the path of the creek that they continued to follow northward. Although it meant weaving between the plentiful saplings, the thick growth helped to protect them from the bitter winter wind. Kiera's legs tired quickly from the extra weight of the snowshoes and the heavy load of the sled. She seemed to be endlessly apologizing to Chocan for their slow pace. Chocan never complained, but he remained unusually quiet, which made Kiera feel even more guilty with each rest break. Although he didn't show it, she could sense that Chocan was worried about making it to the Viking village before mid-spring.

They spent their first night lying on the soft needles of a large pine tree and were well on their way again by the time the first rays of sunlight reached the powdery forest floor. With each day, Kiera felt her strength slowly return. By the end of the week, for the first time since her rescue in the fall, she began to feel like her previously healthy self. Fewer breaks for the duo meant more distance covered. Chocan's mood finally began to lighten.

They spent the long hours on the trail trading tales of the Irish, Norse and Beothuck cultures. What fascinated Chocan the most about the cultures to the east was their ability to use metal.

"So the iron in your needle came from rock?" he asked, intrigued.

"Yes," she explained. "There is a type of rock called iron. If you heat it to a high enough temperature, it melts into a liquid. Then, you pour the purified liquid into a mold and allow it to cool. Once it cools back into a solid, you remove it from the mold, then you're done. The metal tool is complete."

"Incredible," muttered Chocan. "So what other things do you make with this rock called iron?"

Kiera laughed. "I don't know where to begin. First of all, weapons, I suppose. Swords, lances, even arrowheads can all be made with metal. Metal weapons are extremely deadly. I've seen them used firsthand. They can slice through any thickness of leather garment and sever an arm or leg with just one blow. You can see why an army of metal-bearing Vikings can be a formidable foe."

"I now understand the power of these Viking warriors," said Chocan, thoughtfully. "But the Thule do not seem to be frightened of these metal weapons."

"That is because, at the village, the Thule have compensated with overwhelming numbers. We have only twenty-five men in our village. In Ireland, the Vikings would descend upon a village with hundreds of well-armed soldiers. Trust me, if a full armada of Viking ships attacked a Thule village, the only ones left standing would be the Vikings. And the more a village resists, the more ruthless the Vikings become."

Chocan frowned. "We would not be able to

defend ourselves against such an adversary. Our only option, then, would be to avoid contact altogether."

Kiera grimaced at the thought. "I agree. If you see an approaching fleet of Viking ships, my advice would be to run as fast as you can away from their landing site. Viking warriors do not speak with words, but with the sword."

As they came to the summit of a small hill, Chocan pointed northward. A thin trail of smoke rose up from the forest.

"There is the camp. We are close."

"Good," said Kiera, her shoulders sagging. "My legs feel like they are on fire."

He looked over his shoulder and smiled. "For someone who has walked very little in nearly a year, you have done very well. Now let's see if we can reach our brothers and sisters before sundown."

The evening light had almost departed the darkening forest when they entered the northern village. The clearing was empty, but the muffled voices of the band could be heard murmuring through the birch and moss walls of the mamateeks. Chocan shook his head in disgust.

"This must be a village of lazy groundhogs, all tucked away in their little dens for the night. I could have been a Thule warrior and simply walked off with their remaining winter rations. Where is the watch?"

With the silence of a shadow, an arm whipped around Chocan's neck, placing a razor sharp stone against his throat. Kiera gasped in shock at the sudden appearance of a fierce, armed warrior, his narrowed eyes ablaze in anger. She tried to back away, but her snowshoes became tangled in the sled. She landed in a heap upon the wet snow.

Chocan laughed. "You kill me, and you will lose the only person in the Beothuck nation whom you can beat in Chance!"

The grip around Chocan's body softened, and the warrior's face lightened. "You've got a point. I suppose the Creator would want me to take pity on such a pathetic Chance player. How are you, Chocan?"

The warrior removed the knife, stepped in front of him and the two embraced. "Tired. It's good to see you again, Taregan. This is my good friend, Kiera."

Kiera smiled awkwardly from her tangled mess on the ground.

"Hello, I think."

Taregan bent down and stretched out a hand. She took it, and he easily hauled her back up onto her feet.

"I remember you from the Meeting Place. Sorry about the fright, Kiera. Chocan and I go back to when he first arrived in our land."

Chocan shook his head. "I can't believe that you were the first person we met after making the crossing. It's no wonder my sister and I didn't hop back into my canoe and return to Mi'kmaq territory."

Taregan laughed. "I watched Chocan lead his sister aimlessly around the coastal woods. I took pity on such a poor, helpless individual and decided it was safe to introduce them to my band. They stayed with us for over a year, learned our ways, and then, at the Meeting Place, left to be with Nadie's band. Ungrateful, wouldn't you agree?"

"I think, then, that Chocan's come a long way," Kiera said, cheerfully. "He could have deserted me when I was nearly dead, but he saved my life. I owe him everything."

It was then that Taregan noticed, in the fading light, her green eyes behind the layers of red ochre. "I had forgotten that you are not Beothuck. You speak it very well. Much better, in fact, than he ever did after his first year among us."

Chocan shook his head in mock exasperation.

"Thank you," replied Kiera, giggling.

Chocan explained the situation as band members began to spill out of the mamateeks, curious at the commotion. Everyone was surprised to see visitors in winter. Many gathered around, listening to their story of rescue and hopeful repatriation. At the end of the tale, a late-arriving man stepped through the crowd. Tall and cloaked in an impressive skin of wolf, he approached the two strangers.

"I am Rowtag, chief of this band."

Taregan introduced the visitors.

Rowtag frowned. "It is late in winter. Our supplies are low. We have no room in our band for newcomers."

"Do not worry, Rowtag," Chocan replied. "We will not be staying long. In fact, we will continue our journey northwards in the morning, and we will compensate you for our stay. All we ask of you is a place to rest for the night."

"Chocan?" The chief's eyes brightened. "I didn't

recognize you! It has been a long time since we have had a chance to talk."

They embraced. "It's good to see you again as well."

"You are going north?" repeated Rowtag, surprised. "Any further north and you will be entering Thule-controlled land."

Chocan's face dropped. "Have they advanced this far already?"

Rowtag grunted. "They pushed further inland while we were at the Meeting Place. The invaders have taken over our summer camp, near the river's mouth to the Great Water. That is where they are wintering. What my band will do in the spring when it comes time to return to the coast, I do not know."

Chocan thought for a moment. "Send word to Nadie of the situation. I'm sure my band can give you residence until we mount an attack to rid our land of the invaders this summer."

Rowtag clasped Chocan's shoulder. "Thank you."

"How many Thule are residing at your summer camp?" Chocan asked.

"There are not many," added Taregan, "perhaps a couple of dozen. I have seen the cooking smoke from their fires."

Chocan frowned. "This is not good news. First, they invaded and conquered all of the peaceful Tunit villages in the land beyond the north waters, and now they have pushed further into our land. We must repel them before their numbers increase. The tribal council will need to know of this."

"I will meet with the council in the spring and inform them of the worsening situation," agreed Rowtag. "Until we rid our lands of these invaders, it will not be safe for the two of you to go any further north."

"I'm afraid we don't have much choice," Chocan explained. "Kiera needs to get back home."

"Home?" asked Rowtag, noticing for the first time her fair eyes. "And where exactly is that?"

"She needs to go back to the pale strangers' village on the northwest coast of our land," Chocan explained. "The people she calls Viking."

"Ah, the long boat people," he said, staring at Kiera. "We have seen your vessel cross through our bays several times. I have never seen your village, although a Thule captive did talk about it. He said it was a week's paddle north of the Great Bay. Your people have angered the Thule. Their chief's son is dead because of what your people did during an argument several seasons ago. You will never be welcomed by them."

Kiera frowned. "The Thule have already made that perfectly clear. They have been attacking my village for some time. Our leader has decided to leave and return to the Viking lands in the east. I need to get back there before they leave so that I am not left behind."

"Lands to The East?" repeated Rowtag, astonished. "The Vikings come from the Land of the Teachers?"

Kiera explained who she was, who the Vikings and Teachers were, and how she had ended up in this land. After her story, she was thankful that the chief didn't ask why she wanted to go back to Ireland. He just simply nodded, as if he had green-eyed travellers from across the ocean pass through his village on a regular basis.

Calmly, he looked at Chocan, then Kiera. "There is a long and dangerous journey ahead for both of you. Please, stay with us for as long as you need. You will be our honoured guests."

SIXTEEN

Kiera felt as if her body had been trampled by a caribou. Every muscle in her body protested as she pried her eyes open within the smoky confines of the mamateek. The ten-day walk had exhausted her more than she had realized. As her eyes came into focus, she discovered that she was alone. Bright light streamed in through the cracks of the protective leather flap. What time was it? She felt as if she had slept the whole day away.

Quickly bundling herself up, she stepped out into the noonday sun. She blinked until her eyes adjusted to the harsh early spring light. The village was a flurry of activity. She wandered past the women preparing a fish stew, wishing them a good day. She asked if they had seen Chocan. They stared at her with curiosity, then pointed towards the river. She made her way through the playing children, past several men testing out their newly carved spears. After a short jog down a gentle hill, she came to the edge of the river. The body of water was much larger than the creek that ran through Nadie's winter village. The river was already swelling with early run-off, and the centre of the choppy river was clear of ice. Looking downstream, she found Chocan talking with Rowtag under a large pine. Beside them were the village's canoes, sheltered from the ravages of winter.

Chocan pointed to a smaller craft, one that had been built with a shallower draft for navigating the river systems. Most of the other canoes had a deep "V" hull for ocean travel. Listening in, Kiera realized that they were in the middle of negotiations.

"That is our best river canoe," explained the chief. "I cannot part with it."

Chocan dipped deep into his leather bag and pulled out a large, bulging sack.

"Here is enough whale oil to keep your village stocked until the fall. It is worth more than two canoes, and I am willing to part with it for just one."

"We have enough oil," said Rowtag flatly, although Kiera noticed his eyes were sizing up the sack.

"I should not be offering any more," Chocan grumbled, as he reached again into his bag. " The oil is already a far too generous exchange. All I can offer beyond the oil is this."

He held out his palm. In it rested a strange arrow head, larger than any she had seen before.

Chocan passed the stone piece to the chief for examination. "Hmm, a seal arrow head. Very nice. Although yours is of excellent quality, I'm afraid we already have enough arrow heads of this kind for the spring hunt. But there is something that would be of great interest to me."

"What would that be?"

"A Thule harpoon head."

"Harpoon head?" asked Chocan. "What is that?"

"We have seen the Thule use them to catch even the largest of whales. They are a special type of arrowhead that falls off the harpoon shaft once it has embedded itself in the whale. But we have never had the chance to examine one. It is one of their most guarded secrets."

Chocan shook his head. "No, I'm afraid that I can't offer something I have never even seen myself."

The chief folded his arms and frowned. The negotiations had reached an impasse. Neither man had noticed Kiera. She cleared her voice. Both turned in surprise.

"Perhaps I have something of interest to you."

Rowtag eyed her curiously. Chocan stared at her in hope, wondering what she could possibly offer to the negotiations. She bent over, and from the hem of her skirt, removed a small object. She held it up for him to see.

"This is called a needle. It is made of a special stone called iron. It is a sewing tool, and it is much easier to use than your sharp stones. Just put the sinew through the loop at the top of the needle, then pull it through the material. Here, I'll show you something I did a few weeks ago."

She took off her jacket, tying not to shiver as the cool breeze swirled around her exposed arms. She turned the jacket inside out and showed the chief the fine stitches of a repair in the sleeve. The chief gazed admiringly at the stitch work, then at the strange-looking needle. Chocan grinned. He knew they had the man.

"The gift Kiera made for Nadie with this instrument will be the talk of the Meeting Place when you return next summer," Chocan explained. "Just think, you will be able to duplicate the work seen on this garment for all the members of the band. And also think of how much time could be saved by your village."

"I will even teach your band members how to use it," added Kiera.

Chocan stepped towards the chief and folded his arms. "The oil, the arrow head and the needle. It all can be yours in exchange for the one canoe."

Kiera passed him the needle for his inspection. Rowtag rolled the cold metal of the needle between his fingers, studying the strange object. After a moment of contemplation, he slowly nodded his head in agreement.

"You may have the canoe."

Chocan grabbed Kiera's arm in joy. Turning to her, he looked down into her eyes with the happiness of victory.

"Thank you."

She smiled back. "For a way home, it was the least I could do."

* * *

The next morning, the entire band came to the river's edge to watch the foolhardy pair push off from the edge of the near-frozen river. No one had ever dared attempt a canoe trip so early in the spring. The water was simply too high, too fast, and too dangerous. Kiera and Chocan waved to the sombre crowd as the current swiftly guided them downstream.

Chocan, sitting in the stern, expertly guided the craft through the choppy water. His skillful steering wound the canoe around the frothing rocks and downed tree limbs. Kiera did her best to follow his instructions. Following his commands, she would switch from side to side with her paddle, even reverse paddle if a danger appeared unexpectedly. Her strong strokes gave Chocan the momentum he needed to steer the craft even in the fastest-moving water. Her focused concentration helped to keep her mind from reliving the near-death experience that had occurred when she had last stepped into a canoe.

Flying through the high water, the canoe literally launched itself over the edge of the first set of rapids. As the water fell away from the bottom of the craft, Kiera was momentarily airborne. She floated weightlessly with her stomach in her throat before she was rudely pulled back to earth, landing in the gaping mouth of a churning maelstrom. She had to fight her panic as the bow dipped into each frothing hole, only to rocket out the far side through a towering curved wall of water. Her teeth gritted together as sheets of icy spray stung her exposed face and hands.

During a rare calm section of water, she turned to Chocan, her eyes wide and wild, her wet hair plastered to her forehead. The red ochre had been nearly washed clean from her face. Chocan was momentarily stunned by her appearance. He had forgotten how pale and smooth her skin had been when he had first rescued her. Her green eyes twinkled in the glistening early spring air.

"Wouldn't it have been easier to walk?"

"I'm sorry about the rough ride. We would never have been able walk to your village in time. By using a canoe and paddling along the coast, we will take weeks off our trip. Also, to go across land, we would have had to put up with the very unpleasant clouds of blackflies that live in the lower areas. The flies are just a few weeks away from hatching. Even a thick coating of red ochre will not keep them under control. They attack your exposed ears and eyes. They can drive you mad."

"In other words," she sighed, "we had no choice."

He nodded.

"So how many times have you canoed this early in the year?" she asked.

"Never."

"Never," she groaned. "So this really is an adventure to you."

"Life, when it is challenging, stirs the spirit," he replied, smiling.

She was about to bemoan his cheerfulness, but the words were stolen from her mouth. The canoe suddenly disappeared from under her as the river took another monstrous plunge downhill. Chocan laughed as Kiera screamed. The canoe once again rocketed towards the ocean.

SEVENTEEN

I t was not the waning light that brought their voyage towards the sea to a halt, but the frigid, strength-sapping cold of their river-soaked clothes. Together, they were barely able to haul their canoe onto the frozen embankment of the river. They desperately attempted to start a fire in a nearby clearing. Kiera had to will her reluctant limbs to carry an armful of dry twigs and branches back to the camp. Upon arrival, she was dismayed to find Chocan still struggling to start a fire. His fingers were so numb that the flint fell from his hand whenever he tried to strike it with the stone.

"Would you like me to try?" she asked, putting down the sticks.

He held the stones up to her. "I'm sorry. My hands are useless."

Before she took the stones from him, she wrapped her hands around his fingers. "Chocan, your fingers are like ice! Stick them inside your coat and under your armpits. You don't want to risk frostbite."

Chocan did as he was told. Kiera knelt down, placed the rocks above the bits of dry moss and began striking the stones together. On the fifth hit, several sparks fell onto the moss. She continued to spray the moss with sparks until she saw the tiniest trickle of smoke. Putting the rocks on her lap, she leaned forward and began to blow gently on the tinder. The smoke thickened until a small orange flame licked the air. Chocan managed to pass her several tiny pieces of bark, and together they nursed the tiny glow into a roaring campfire.

After removing their wet outer clothes and replacing them with a second set of dry garments, they hung up their wet clothes on a branch that hung over the fire, then huddled together under a thick, caribou blanket, allowing the fire and their combined body heat to calm their uncontrollable shivering.

It was an hour before they had regained enough control over their numbed bodies to continue setting up camp. Kiera organized the sleeping area for the night while Chocan speared several fish, then roasted them on a wet, wooden grill over the open flames. As they ate, their strength returned. Kiera gazed out to the river.

"How long do you think it will take to get back to my village?"

My village. The words echoed in Chocan's mind. He sighed and looked into her distant eyes that stared beyond him and into the future. As they travelled, her Beothuck spirit, like the ochre that had been cleansed from her face, was slowly being washed away. He joined her gaze toward the water. The fast-running river that was carrying them ever closer to the sea was itself the portal between their worlds. He now realized that she would not be able to exist in both. It wrenched his heart, but he knew he would have to let her go.

"We have made good progress."

Kiera waited for more, yet Chocan remained silent. She sensed an uneasy feeling that she had never felt before with her friend. Something was wrong. She leaned forward and touched his shoulder.

"What is it, Chocan?"

He turned to her, lost in his own thoughts. "I'm sorry?"

"Is there something wrong?"

"I don't know what you mean."

"Yes, you do. You're thinking about something. I feel like your mind is on the other side of the world."

"Not quite the other side."

She looked at him quizzically. "What's that supposed to mean?"

"I was thinking about the world to which you are returning. You are allowing yourself to lose your freedom and once again become a slave."

Her face hardened. "You don't think that I've had sleepless nights over that thought? Even though I have considerate masters, they still are not my family. They bought me at an auction and took me away from my home. I thought you understood. If I knew that Thorfinn and the other Vikings were planning to stay here in your land permanently, then I would not hesitate to turn my back on them. I would gladly start my life anew with you and your band."

Chocan slid closer to her. "But you have been away from your home for so many years. Even if you do somehow manage to get back to Ireland, there is a possibility that your family will no longer be at your childhood home. They may have been captured or killed in other raids. They may have left the area to avoid further attack. Perhaps Ireland itself won't be the same, after so many years of Viking rule. The home you remember may no longer exist. Will all of this effort and agony that you are now choosing to endure be for nothing?"

In her exhaustion, she could feel her dream shattering with each word. A tear trickled down her cheek. "Why are you saying this to me? Weeks ago, you said that I should follow my heart!"

"I'm only trying to prepare you for what you might find," he replied. "I owe you, as a friend, to help you think this through. You will be giving up many things, including your freedom. If you have any doubts, you should consider them now. Tomorrow we leave Beothuck territory. Given the weather, it will be very difficult to turn back."

She reached over and took his hand in her palms. "I know you are only trying to help. But Chocan, I need to try. I need to get back to the Viking village."

Chocan smiled. "If your family is anything like you, then I think they will be looking for you with the same ferocity that burns within your heart. You are choosing the path to which you have been called."

Kiera smiled. "Thank you."

Chocan collapsed onto the mattress of pine needles and closed his eyes. "I understand your feelings more than you realize. I, too, sometimes long for home. My village, where I was raised and born, will always be a part of me. In a way, the village of the Teachers is like stepping onto the soil of Ireland. After all, the Irish teachers created it. And it is also a distant home. It may remain forever beyond my reach."

Kiera was surprised. She thought about Chocan's words. They were more similar than she had ever realized.

"I'm sorry, Chocan. I had never known you felt that way. So tell me, why can't you return home?"

She looked at Chocan, but he had already drifted off to sleep. The fire crackled and popped beside her, calling out for more fuel. Her heart felt as if it were being torn in different directions. She searched within the flames for a hidden message, a direction amid the chaotic light. The flames once again danced the Irish jigs and crackled to the beat of the Celtic drums. Closing her weary eyes, she was lulled to sleep by the music of the dance.

EIGHTEEN

The next day was the warmest of the early spring. The added heat was a welcome present to the soggy travellers. The warmth of the sun, however, added to the height of the run-off, which was foremost in their minds as they careened their way over more treacherous sets of rapids. But the rapids were now becoming far and few between. Kiera and Chocan attacked the longer stretches of calm water with their paddles. Their effort helped to loosen their cold, tired muscles.

Another night and day saw the river gradually widen into a mature channel which carved its way through a steep, narrow gorge. A week later, Kiera was awestruck as the river opened up even further into a long, narrow bay, with either shore guarded by enormous, curved mountains that seemed to stretch right up to the clouds above. Tufts of green shoots were already beginning to sprout up along the icy shore.

Kiera stopped paddling and soaked in the scene. "Incredible."

Chocan also paused. "I have seen this place only once before, when I came north to trade with the Tunit."

"Were they the northern people that the Thule conquered a few years ago?"

"Yes. The Thule are, if nothing else, efficient warriors."

Kiera looked skywards towards the feathery, afternoon clouds. The warm sun revitalized her spirits. In the distance, she caught sight of a black mother bear leading her cubs to the edge of water. The young bears jumped into the chilly water, splashing each other with their furry paws. Suddenly, the mother bear stiffened. A low grunt made the cubs freeze as well. The animals jumped out of the water and scampered for the safety of the forest. Something had frightened them. Kiera thought she caught something move near the mouth of a small river where the bears were playing.

"Chocan, what's that?" She pointed with her paddle.

Chocan allowed the canoe to drift as he scanned the shoreline.

"Oh, no."

Kiera squinted into the fading afternoon sunset. A flash, like a fish breaching the water, caught her eye. A small craft. Then, a second craft appeared from the shore, followed by several more. They were all paddling hard. They were coming after them!

"Kayaks!" Chocan shouted. "They were not supposed to be this far inland. Start paddling! We have to get to the far shore!"

Chocan heaved hard on the stern paddle. Kiera dug into the water with all of her might, and the canoe turned away from the approaching boats.

"Thule?" Kiera asked.

"Thule," Chocan grunted as they both paddled for their lives.

Kiera's blisters from days of paddling were quickly forgotten. She ripped at the water, the muscles of her shoulders and arms bulging from the effort. The water peeled away from the cutting bow as the craft lurched forward with each pull. They aimed their canoe at a wooded point that jutted out into the deep fjord. With the cover of the trees, they could then escape the attack on foot. She glanced over her shoulder. The kayaks were gaining. Each boat had a single paddler. The boats themselves were low in the water, barely visible above the gentle chops of the inlet. But she could clearly see behind each paddler a spear or bow pointing skyward. The attackers were yelling at them in a very unfriendly way.

"I don't know if we're going to make it. Their kayaks are much faster than our canoe."

"There's only one way to find out," he grunted. "Keep paddling!"

"Should I dig out our bow and arrow?"

"No. There are too many of them. If we try to defend ourselves, they will kill us. Escape is our only hope."

There was no point in looking back again. Kiera focused on the far shore. She willed the trees to reach out and bring their fragile canoe into the protection of their sheltering limbs. The forest itself seemed to shout words of encouragement. They were so close now, she could see the perfect muddy spot on which to beach the craft and make a dash for the forest.

A yelp of pain broke Kiera's concentration. Chocan's face was contorted in agony, his back arched. One hand reached over his shoulder, wildly grasping for something. When he turned, she gasped. An arrow was lodged in his back, just below his right shoulder. Past Chocan, she saw the eight kayaks. The nearest Thule grinned, the bow still in his hand.

In anger, Kiera dove into the bottom of the canoe. She ripped her weapon out from under the leather bags and was about to load it with an arrow when Chocan put his foot on top of the buried quiver.

"No," he moaned through clenched teeth. "You mustn't. Pick up your paddle and slowly wave it back and forth."

Every angry fibre in Kiera's body willed her to fight back, to ignore his plea and to start firing arrows at the tormentors of not only her people, but the Beothuck as well. But a higher calm slowly washed over her. Chocan was her friend. She trusted his judgment. She took a deep breath, sat back down and picked up the paddle. She waved it slowly over her head.

It took only a moment for the canoe to be encircled by the fast-moving kayaks. A man with a thick, dark moustache and craggy face started yelling fiercely at them. Kiera put down the paddle. Chocan answered back in a language she didn't understand. The Thule replied with less anger and paddled closer to the canoe.

Chocan looked to Kiera. "He wants us to paddle

back to their camp. When I told him that I could no longer paddle, he told me to move into the middle of the canoe. He will paddle in the stern."

Chocan awkwardly crawled into the centre of the canoe. When Kiera turned to Chocan in an attempt to help him with the arrow, more angry shouts erupted, and several spears and arrows were aimed directly at her.

"Kiera," Chocan moaned, "this is important. Don't do anything unless I say so, and that includes helping me. They must believe that we won't cause any trouble. If they feel that we will fight back or try to escape, they won't hesitate to kill us. Do you understand?"

She nodded. The Thule climbed into the back of the canoe, and after tying the kayak to the stern of the canoe, he commanded her with gestures to start paddling. It was a solemn crossing under a darkening sky. Kiera was overwhelmed with fear and anger. She was not upset with her own capture but furious at herself for dragging Chocan into this mess. He lay behind her, injured, bound and deflated. How could she have done such a thing to the person who had so bravely saved her life?

The small armada of vessels pulled onto the far shore in the inky darkness of a moonless night. Their only beacon, a campfire, was roaring with life. The Thule disembarked and, with spears in hand, prodded Kiera and Chocan away from their canoe and up the slight rise to the circle of skin tents. Kiera scanned the crowd. Only men were present at the campfire gathering. The triumphant Thule hunters laughed and bantered with those who had remained behind, relaying the tale of the capture.

Kiera stared at the ground, trying to pretend she was anywhere else but here. She once again felt as if she was a prize to be fought over, as she was poked and pushed by the hunters. Memories of that horrible auction in Iceland flooded her mind. For the first time, she wondered what might happen to her. The thought of being considered property to such volatile men drove a knife of fear deep into her stomach.

The leader of the camp, the man who had paddled the canoe with her, grabbed Kiera roughly by the arm and dragged her closer to the fire for all to see. Her ochre had long been washed away. Even in the orange light of the fire, her green eyes glowed like sunlit emeralds. Her shimmering auburn hair framed her pale, worried face. The men gawked, her pale skin bringing a gasp of astonishment. Kiera shuffled her feet uncomfortably, trying to control the urge to elbow the leader in the stomach, grab Chocan and make a run for the darkened meadow.

A shorter man, from the opposite side of the fire, stepped forward. He stared at her in a different, more curious way than the astonished gapes of his comrades. He slowly circled around the burning logs and moved closer. Kiera's lowered eyes noticed the approaching legs. She willed herself to look up at the approaching stranger. Her eyes widened in shock. The artwork on his face was that of a mighty eagle's wing. He stopped in front of her, his nose almost touching hers. She could smell the evening meal of fish fried in fat in his sour breath. She tried to turn away, but the leader's grasp of her arm suddenly increased to the point where she yelped in pain. The shorter man roughly grabbed her under the jaw. He held her astonished face in a vice-like grip as he inspected her closely. Trapped, Kiera could feel a deep anger rise within her. Cool and defiant, she stared back into the eyes of her enemy. There was no doubt in her mind. He was the Thule that she had captured in the Viking village.

A sly smile spread across the warrior's face. He bent down towards the fire and picked something up off the ground. Kiera finally breathed as the warrior stepped away from her, retracing his route back around the campfire.

Then, with lightning speed, he pivoted, spun and swung. In the corner of her eye, she saw something racing towards her head, but being firmly held, there was nothing she could do. In an explosion of light, Kiera felt her world spinning in a whirlpool, down towards an unending darkness.

Kiera collapsed in a heap. Her attacker gazed with satisfaction at the crumpled young woman on the ground, gently tapping the log that he had used to attack her in his other palm. A bitter grin touched his lips as he turned and threw the wood onto the roaring fire, then walked away.

NINETEEN

Kiera fought through the unending waves of pain and nausea. Her head felt as if it had been split wide open. She tried to touch the throbbing wound beside her left eye, but to her dismay, her hand was not free to investigate. Her wrists were firmly secured behind her back.

Moaning, Kiera managed to squint into the bright light. She was surprised to find herself in the bottom of a ribbed, skin-covered boat. She also became aware of the rise and fall of the sea. Where was she? A rush of panic swept over her as she tried to recall what had happened, but her last memory was of paddling with Chocan through the majestic fjord. What was going on? She began to thrash against her bindings, dangerously rocking the skin-covered vessel. Someone yelled at her in a strange tongue.

"Stop moving," said a soothing voice in her native Irish tongue. "You don't want to upset him again."

She tilted her head back and saw an upside-down but concerned face. Chocan, also tied and bound, was wedged in behind her. Together, they took up almost the entire rear of the small vessel. The memories of last night slowly returned. She looked forward. The Thule who had attacked her sat on a bench just beyond her head. He was paddling with his back to them. A coat of caribou with a fur-lined hood hung from his shoulders. Bags and clothing were stored between his knees and the bow.

She looked back to Chocan. "Where are we?"

"We are being transported back to the Thule homeland. This warrior here thinks that, despite your previous encounters, he can mold you into a fine wife. He seems to be quite taken by your green eyes. He has decided that you are to live with his other wife and children back on the Thule mainland."

Kiera gritted her teeth in anger. "Marry him? Good luck to that ever happening. What about you? Is he going to marry you as well?"

Chocan managed a smile. "If only I were so lucky. No, they have decided that I might be useful, since both the Thule and I understand the Tunit language. In exchange for my life, they want me to help plan future raids against the Beothuck."

"Oh, is that all?" groaned Kiera. "How long have I been unconscious, Chocan?"

"About a day now. We left the camp at daybreak, and he has been paddling ever since. I would guess we are about a quarter of the way up the northwest coast of our island. Another week of paddling, then a journey across the northern strait, and we will be in the heart of Thule territory."

"How's your shoulder?" she asked, looking concerned.

"It's been better," he answered, grimacing at the thought of his wound.

"Don't aggravate it. Stay put while I take a look around."

Kiera tried to sit up, but Chocan shook his head in alarm.

"I wouldn't recommend it. I've already tried. He said if I moved, he would do to me with the log what he had already done to you. 'Either way,' he said, 'you will lie still on the bottom of the craft.'"

"Speaking of craft," said Kiera. "I've never seen one like this. It's different from the kayaks that attacked us earlier."

"It's what the Thule call an inuak. It's about the size of a Beothuck canoe with an open top, but it sits lower in the water. They use it for hauling cargo. "

A thought struck Kiera. "So the three of us are out here all alone?"

Chocan shook his head. "No. Four other kayaks are travelling with us. Each kayak is towing a newly-made empty kayak back to their homeland. Besides scouting out territory in order to plan further hostilities against us, they spent their free time during the evenings making more kayaks."

Kiera pondered their situation. "Did you learn anything from the Thule last night?"

"They mentioned your village."

Her eyes widened. "They did?"

"Our wing-faced friend here explained why he had hit you. It was in retaliation for you doing the same to him last summer. They went on to talk about the peace offering that your leader had proposed. It appears the idea of allowing your people to leave peacefully has split the Thule leadership. Some want to let your village leave peacefully and be done with it. Others still want revenge for past deaths in battle. These men are part of the group that want to seek revenge. They are deliberately ignoring the orders of their chief. They plan to attack your Viking village again with a large number of men in ten days. The empty kayaks we are pulling behind us are to be used by the warriors. From what I have overheard, the numbers in this attack are going to be overwhelming. Over a hundred armed Thule warriors. Your Viking friends may not get that opportunity to return home."

"Ten days!" exclaimed Kiera, shocked. "We've got to..."

Kiera's assailant turned around, his face furious. He yelled at them both.

Chocan whispered. "He said he liked you better when you were unconscious. He told us to be quiet or else."

Kiera, unwavering, returned a defiant look, but remained silent. Wing-Face flashed a cruel smile at the helpless woman, then returned to his paddling. Kiera leaned her sore head on the curve of Chocan's comforting calves. She tried to claw her thoughts above the constant throbbing in her brain. They couldn't give up. But what could they do? They were tied and bound, floating with a vicious warrior in a boat no bigger than a canoe.

She glanced down at her skirt. An idea struck her. Could it still be there? Slowly hiking up the skirt with her bound hands, she managed to reach the hem. Chocan watched her, his eyes widening with hope. Feeling her way along the material, her fingers finally touched its cold, narrow surface. She delicately removed her last needle from its resting place.

Twisting her wrists until the pain was almost unbearable, she aimed the needle at the leather strips between her hands. She then began to poke, over and over again, in the same location of the leather. Twice, she had to quickly hide the needle in her palm as their captor swung around to check on them. He seemed satisfied that his prisoners were behaving themselves and went back to the task of guiding the craft towards his homeland.

The sun hung low on the horizon. She knew they would soon be stopping for the night. Kiera continued to poke the leather. Her fingers were now so sore and raw that she was afraid she might drop the needle. When a drop of blood dripped from her fingertip onto the ribbing of the inuak, she knew that it was time to stop. She palmed the needle and took a deep breath. Gritting her teeth, she silently pulled against the leather straps with all of her strength. Her shoulders strained with effort. Nothing. She tried again. Her wrists began to burn with pain. She made a third attempt. A slight snap tickled their ears. Relaxing, she looked back at Chocan. He looked at her wrists and nodded encouragement. Taking the needle once again, she again worked feverishly on the same section of leather.

A minute later, she tried again. This time, a louder snap greeted her effort. She froze. Had Wing-Face heard the noise? She slowly lifted her eyes. Thankfully, he continued paddling, oblivious to what was going on behind him. Kiera quickly removed the leather straps from around her wrists then undid her legs. She quietly leaned her head back on Chocan's lap and released his wrists and ankles. Using hand signals and silent gestures, they put together their plan.

Kiera quietly twisted until she was on her hands and knees behind Wing-Face. Chocan leaned forward, using Kiera's back for support, until he was within arm's reach of the Thule warrior. Wing-Face must have felt the shift in weight because his head began to turn. In a lightning move, Chocan grabbed him hard around the chest and face. His hand slapped over Wing-Face's mouth to prevent a shout of warning to the others. Chocan then yanked the shocked warrior over Kiera's back, ignoring the paddle as it fell overboard, and allowed Wing-Face to fall hard onto his chest. Kiera grabbed the floating paddle and threw it back into the bow of the boat. Wing-Face, coming to his senses, began to struggle, but Kiera sprang like a cat and threw her whole weight behind her elbow, crashing it into the Thule's unprotected stomach. Wing-Face's eyes spread wide with pain as the wind was knocked out of his lungs. Chocan took advantage of the situation by releasing the Thule's mouth. He quickly gagged him with a thick piece of leather. Kiera, meanwhile, pinned his arms with her knees. Chocan slipped out from underneath Wing-Face, and together they tied him up.

Kiera scrambled up onto the seat. Had the others seen the skirmish? She gave a sigh of relief. Instead of looking up into the tip of an angry spear-holding Thule warrior, she saw the other four kayaks well out ahead of them. The Thule had their backs to the slower craft, and they were unaware of the scenario taking place behind them. She scanned the surroundings for a hiding place. To her dismay, they were in the middle of a huge bay that she had remembered crossing during the morning of their second day of sailing. The coast was far away to her right. She looked over her shoulder. Beyond the kayak they were towing, the southeastern tip of the bay was but a mere smudge on the horizon. With water in every direction, hiding was not an option. They needed another plan.

"Any ideas?" asked Kiera.

Chocan looked around the open water. "I suggest we get as far away from the other kayaks as possible."

Kiera picked up the paddle. "I agree. You're injured. I'll do the paddling."

Kiera turned the inuak around and started paddling hard towards the southwest tip of the bay.

"We've come further than I thought," he said, noting the coastline.

"What about the other kayaks?"

He looked over his shoulder. "They still have not noticed our change in direction."

"That's not going to last. Any ideas on how to improve our slim odds?"

Chocan bent over and lay down in the bottom of the boat beside the Thule.

"If they see two of us sitting upright, they will definitely know there is a problem."

"All right," she said, glancing over her shoulder, "that's a good idea. But they are still close enough to us to see that I'm not Thule."

Chocan grabbed the hood of the Thule's jacket and tore it from the rest of the coat. Their prisoner, realizing what they were up to, began to thrash in anger. Chocan placed the hood on top of Kiera's head.

"The hood might be enough to fool them, at least for a little while. With a bit of luck, they might think that our friend has forgotten something, or is in need of a minor repair. Perhaps they won't bother to investigate the situation."

"Well," she grunted between pulls, "if it's all right with you, I'll just keep paddling with everything I've got."

"By all means," replied Chocan, keeping low.

He poked his head up and over the stern to keep an eye on the kayaks. Kiera was starting to believe that their escape might end up being smooth after all. But their luck didn't hold.

"Uh-oh."

Chocan stared at a changing scene behind them. The four kayaks had stopped. Three of the warriors had untied their unmanned kayaks from their sterns and passed the tow ropes to the single, remaining kayak. Free of their burden, the trio of warriors then turned around and began to chase the inuak.

"What's happening?"

"I'm afraid we have been discovered."

Kiera turned to check out the dire situation. She threw the itchy hood into the bow.

"Any ideas now?"

Chocan reached over the stern, grabbed the tow line and pulled. Within seconds, their empty kayak was bobbing alongside their inuak. Chocan took a deadly harpoon in his right hand, then cut the ties that had bound the captured Thule's legs with his left.

"Get in," he commanded in Tunit.

But the Thule didn't move. He simply glared back at him with an icy smile. Chocan moved a harpoon and placed the sharp tip against his chest.

"Get into the kayak, or you will soon be swimming home."

The smile disappeared, and the Thule reluctantly climbed into the kayak. Without his arms, he nearly tipped the craft, but Chocan helped him collapse onto its ribbed hull. Chocan cut the tow rope. With guidance from only the wind and waves, the kayak began to drift out to sea.

"That should help us go a little faster," said Chocan.

Kiera grimaced. "I can't say that I'll miss my husband-to-be."

"Since our winged friend doesn't have a paddle, someone will have head out to sea and rescue him. It may force those who are chasing us to split up."

Kiera tried to clear her thoughts and concentrate on her paddling. Chocan would have been a much stronger paddler, but with his injured shoulder, she realized that it would be up to her to get them to safety. Her wrists were still sore from being tied, but otherwise her arms were well-rested. The exertion, however, caused her injured head to throb like a bass drum. She heaved against the water with each stroke, frustrated that the distant ribbon of land ahead of her seemed frozen to the horizon. She knew their chances of escape were slim. But the horrid thought of being married to her Thule captor gave her all the motivation she needed to give each stroke a superhuman effort.

"It looks like our plan worked," said Chocan. "One of the kayaks did go after our friend. Now there are only two chasing us."

Kiera stole a glance over her shoulder. "I'm getting a bad feeling about this. The kayaks are smaller, lighter and faster than us, and it is still a long paddle back to the point. Even if we make it to land, there is nowhere to hide. They will be chasing us over marsh and barren rock."

Chocan looked up at the sky. "Actually, we don't need to make it to shore. We just have to stay ahead of them for a little while longer."

"Why?" Kiera grunted.

"The sun is almost touching the horizon. Soon, darkness will fall. It will also be a moonless night. Once night falls, they will never find us on the open ocean. The Thule are excellent ocean kayakers and hunters, but without the moon, they will be as blind as moles."

"Uh, Chocan, I hate to tell you this, but so will we."

"Our plan right now is simply to survive so that we can see another day. If it means drifting in the ocean all night, then so be it."

Kiera glanced over her shoulder again. Already she could see that the kayaks were gaining on them.

"I don't think we'll last even to see the sun kiss the horizon. They're simply too fast."

Chocan assessed the situation. "They are only human. They have been paddling against the wind all day. They have to be tired. Our advantage is our rested state. We will switch as soon as you cannot keep up this pace."

"But you're injured!" Kiera protested.

He shrugged. "Better an injured paddler than an exhausted one."

Chocan began to dig through the supplies left in the bottom of the inuak. To make the craft lighter and faster, he tossed overboard three coils of leather twine, most of the stored food, some tools and almost all of the water bags. Kiera's eyes widened as she saw Chocan getting ready to throw some large caribou skins overboard.

"Chocan! Stop! I have an idea. I think my arms have had it anyway. How do you suggest we switch?"

"Spread your feet apart," he replied. "I'm going to go under your seat."

After crawling under Kiera and into the front of the boat, Kiera wiggled back on her seat as far as she could go. Chocan then rose up between the paddle and Kiera until he was sitting on the front edge of the seat between her legs. She let Chocan grab the paddle as she slid off the back of the seat and landed in the stern. They barely missed a stroke.

"Nice transfer," said Kiera, stretching her shoulders.

"So what's the plan?" asked Chocan.

"I'll show you in a minute."

Kiera bent down to examine the items still remaining on the floor of the boat. She again removed the needle from her hem and began to tear apart the bottom of her filthy skirt. She removed the long threads that held together the hem and placed them in a pile between her knees. She then threw the edge of the largest skin over the harpoon pole and quickly sewed the corners of the skin into pockets. She made an even larger pocket in the skin exactly halfway along the length of the pole. Finding a second, similar-sized skin, she ignored the fiery pain and dripping blood from her fingertips as she sewed the two skins together, end to end. She could only hope that the stitching would be strong enough.

Now she needed some leather twine. She dug around the remaining items. Then she remembered Chocan had already thrown the twine overboard! Desperately, she looked around for an alternative. Her winter mukluks! She pulled the laces from both boots and tied them in a knot to make an even longer lace.

She eyed Chocan's feet. "I'll need your laces as well."

Chocan didn't argue. In a flash, she was under

his seat. She tied the laces together, then went to work attaching each lace to the free corners of the skins. Finally, it was finished. She was so engrossed with her work that she had not bothered to look behind her. The scene sent a chill down her back. The Thule kayaks were so close that she could see the beads of perspiration on their exhausted but determined faces. It was only a matter of moments before they would be within the range of the Thule weapons.

Kiera turned back to Chocan. Her eyes went wide in shock. The back of his leather coat was stained dark red, while a crimson pool of blood gathered under his seat between the ribs of the skin hull.

"Chocan, your shoulder!"

"They're going to catch us," he gasped, "aren't they?"

"Not if my idea works."

Kiera looked around at the rolling ocean waves. The dark, forbidding surface was choppy, but would it be enough?

"What do you want me to do?"

"When I say," explained Kiera, "I want you to give me the end of the paddle. I'll stick it into the middle pocket of the skin. Then you will have to raise it up off your shoulder and brace it against the thwart and the rib on the floor ahead of you."

He nodded, too tired to reply.

Kiera took a deep breath. "All right. Let's do it."

Although exhausted and in pain, Chocan somehow managed to swing the paddle tip behind him and onto his shoulder. The tip landed right on her lap. Slipping the paddle into her sewn creation, she was relieved to see that the pocket made a perfect fit for the paddle. She let go of the leather sheets and grabbed hold of the laces.

"Go, Chocan! Lift the paddle!"

Using his shoulder like a lever, Chocan raised the end of the paddle up towards the sky, transforming it into a makeshift mast. With the harpoon holding the top corners of the blanket apart, the northern wind blew the stretched skins into a beautiful rectangular sail. The stiff breeze tried to rip the leather laces from Kiera's hands, but she was ready for the power of the wind. She had wrapped the laces twice around her wrists and braced her foot against the back of Chocan's seat. She yelped as the pain from her injured wrists raced up her arms. She leaned back and worked the sail right and left in order to maximize the power of the wind. It wasn't a big sail, and she was worried that the strength of the wind would not be enough to match the speed of the smaller kayaks.

"What's happening behind us, Chocan?"

Chocan tore his amazed stare away from the sail and turned back towards their pursuers.

"Your skin cloud is working, Kiera, but I'm afraid they are still gaining, just not as quickly. The closest Thule is reaching for his bow."

Kiera looked to her right. For the first time that day, a smile spread across her face. A frothy disturbance raced towards them like a school of charging fish. A gust of wind was nearly upon them.

"Hold on!" she shouted.

Kiera braced herself as the gust hit the sail. Both she and Chocan grunted from the impact. The inuak suddenly lurched forward, and Kiera could hear the water begin to race past the hull. She closed her eyes and prayed that the sail would stay in one piece. The powerful wind lasted only for a few minutes. As the pressure on the sail eased, Kiera dared another look over her shoulder. The distance between them had nearly doubled.

But with the calming came a second charge from the kayaks. As the Thule once again closed the gap between the crafts, another gust materialized from the north. Kiera and Chocan skimmed through the water, moving beyond the reach of the kayaks. The sky darkened to an indigo twilight. Night had finally fallen.

The Thule shouted some final parting words that Chocan chose not to translate, then broke off their pursuit, turning north. Their captives had escaped. Chocan carefully lowered the sail. They wrapped their arms around each other in wild excitement.

"I can't believe we did it!"

"You did it," corrected Chocan. "The skin cloud... I have never seen a craft, other than a Viking ship, use one before. Your idea saved our lives."

Kiera pressed her hand against his back, and he winced. She felt something warm and sticky. She had forgotten about his injury.

"Your wound! Take off your coat. Let me see it."

Grimacing, Chocan struggled to remove his coat. His lower back was smeared in blood. The arrow from the day before had caught him just below the shoulder blade. The paddling had torn open the wound once again. It thankfully did not appear to be too deep, and his breathing was not affected. Kiera sighed with relief. It was a painful injury, but one that would eventually heal. Kiera washed the wound with salt water, then using leather strips, bandaged the wound.

While being treated, Chocan looked at the wind then to the barely visible coast. "The cloth cloud will take us further away from your village. We will need to use the paddle now in order to move towards shore."

"You have done enough for one day," she said, gently pushing him off the seat. "Let's switch places, and I'll take over the paddling."

Chocan didn't argue. He crawled onto the pile of caribou skins and fell immediately asleep. Kiera looked back at him with concern. Had he been up since yesterday, tending to her in the Thule camp while she lay unconscious? Had he lost too much blood from his wound? Her heart ached as she looked at the man who had become her closest friend, perhaps because she knew that she would have to say goodbye to him very soon. There was so much she wanted to tell him. Now she could only hope that he would survive his injury.

She pulled the paddle out of the makeshift sail and stored the sewn leather and harpoon by her feet. After scanning the horizon one last time for lingering kayaks, she picked out a star to the east, dug the paddle into the rolling Atlantic Ocean and set off for the coast.

TWENTY

Lorna watched in dismay as the bright black and orange butterfly released its grip on her finger and fluttered awkwardly away, zigzagging over the river and toward the inviting meadow beyond. Earlier that spring, she had captured the striped caterpillar, and every day, she had fed the creature handfuls of its favourite leaves. She had secretly hoped that if she treated the creature with love and care, it would someday choose to stay with her and be her friend. Lorna watched in amazement as it wove and hid itself in a tightly wrapped cocoon. For a week, the creature had remained dormant. Then, this morning, it had begun to wiggle free from its prison. Finally, she had a friend to play with! But after stretching out its wings in the sun, the butterfly turned away from its human friend and fluttered off into the morning breeze. Lorna's face wilted in sadness as the creature faded into the background of the colourful spring meadow. Why did all of her friends have to leave? First, it was saying goodbye to the other children in Greenland. Then, Kiera didn't return with the men in the battered ship. She flopped down onto the grass in despair. She had never felt so alone.

Dagmar looked up from her scrubbing on the riverbank and felt for her daughter. The unhappiness in her child's eyes made her heart ache. It had been almost a year since Lorna had become withdrawn. She thought back to the day when Bjorn had returned in the nearly destroyed longboat and told the shocked village of Kiera's death. Confused, Lorna had pushed past her father and the other sailors. She had searched every nook and cranny of the ship for her friend, convinced that it was all an elaborate game of hide and seek. Finally, her father had to physically remove his daughter from the longboat, the villagers staring silently as the young girl pleaded for her friend to come out of hiding.

Dagmar had tried everything to snap Lorna out of her year-long state of melancholy, but nothing had worked. She sighed as she wiped her brow with her apron and returned to her scrubbing. Perhaps leaving this cursed Vinland and returning to Greenland would be the best thing for Lorna. Everywhere, it seemed, sadness had been etched into this deceptively beautiful land. Until they climbed onto the ships for the long sail back east, they would all have to immerse themselves in hard work to keep the ever-present ghosts at bay.

"Momma, can I go see the goats in the pasture?"

Dagmar looked up. "After you fetch the kindling I asked you to get earlier this morning."

Lorna frowned. "Yes, Momma."

"Don't go beyond the boundaries," Dagmar reminded her.

"Yes, Momma."

Lorna trudged off into the thicker grass, heading towards a thin glade of rustling poplars that grew along the river's edge. She half-heartedly picked up several twigs, then glanced across to the far side of the water for perhaps a final glimpse of her flying friend. As she looked up, something peculiar caught her eye.

At the far edge of the meadow, where the river curved back to the sea, Lorna saw a sudden flash of light. Curious, she stopped and stared to see if it would happen again. Nothing. Had it been her imagination? She was about to return to her collecting duties when she saw a second flash, this time much closer.

The flash was accompanied by a voice. It was a faint voice, but strangely familiar. It was the voice that had haunted her dreams for nearly a year. There was somebody coming up the river! Breaking her parents' most important rule, she crossed the village boundary line and eagerly fought through the barrier of thorns and stinging nettles that guarded the river's edge.

*   *   *

The warning call came from Gunnar. He was perched halfway up the mast of the last dry-docked ship. His eyes had also caught the flash from the river. Full of trepidation, he cupped his hands and yelled towards the village.

"Skraelings!"

The warning crackled throughout the village.

Everyone dropped what they were doing and scrambled to their defensive positions. A deadly fight was about to begin. The men working on the ships left their tools and sprinted for the longhouses and their weapons within. The women gathered up their children and herded them into the back corner of the central longhouse. In all the pandemonium, no one heard the distant call of a woman's voice.

Dagmar, frantically pacing the edge of the village boundary, screamed in panic.

"Lorna! Where are you? Lorna!"

Terrified, she turned and ran back into the village. There she saw Thorfinn, who was organizing the men into battle groups. Hysterically, she shook his arm so hard that she nearly flipped the helmet off his head.

"Dagmar, what..."

"Lorna! She's missing! She's gone! Help, please! If the skraelings get her, I don't know what I'll do!"

Thorfinn grabbed Dagmar firmly by the shoulders. "Dagmar, calm down. I promise that we'll find Lorna before we do anything else. Where did you last see her?"

"Over there! At...at the edge of the meadow," she stammered, pointing with a trembling finger. "She was out gathering kindling."

He spun around to face the other armed men. "All right everyone, listen! Lorna is missing! Magnus and Gunnar, you come with me. We're going after her. The rest of you need to fall back to your defensive positions. We'll join you as soon as we can."

The gathering broke up as three men sprinted

towards the edge of the meadow. Thorfinn knew that time was not on his side. If it was a large skraeling assault, then the villagers would be hopelessly outnumbered. Having three of their best fighters away from their positions could make the difference between a victory and an unthinkable disaster.

The men came to a halt at the wall of vegetation that marked the village boundary. Thorfinn scanned the area. On a nearby thorn bush, he spied a tiny piece of cloth. From there, a trail of bent foliage led towards the edge of the river. Without further hesitation, the three men tore through the stinging grasses, hoping it would not be too late.

*   *   *

"Hello! It's me, Kiera! I'm returning with a friend. Please, don't be alarmed!"

Kiera continued her calling, hoping that the village would hear the familiar Nordic language and not panic at their arrival. She knew the village was just around the next bend. She also knew that the villagers would be on edge, worrying about another attack now that spring had returned. She fought her nervousness and continued to call. Perhaps the worst had already occurred. Perhaps she was too late. Her stomach tightened as she contemplated the possibility that the Vikings had already left for Greenland without her.

It had taken Kiera and Chocan eleven days to paddle along the camouflaged confines of the western coast to the mouth of the Viking river. It was a longer and less direct route, but it had reduced the chances of further contact with the Thule. Had their safer route resulted in her missing the departure?

Kiera refused to give up hope. Both she and Chocan had come so far. In her excitement, however, Kiera had forgotten about the ochre. Her hair and body were slathered in the red pigment that now felt like her second skin. It had served its purpose in preventing the worst of the blackfly swarms from feeding upon her as they travelled through the marshy shorelines. It never occurred to her that she should have looked at her own reflection before entering the river.

*   *   *

Lorna stood at the edge of the steep overhang and stared at the approaching craft. Her eyes focused on what looked like a woman standing in the front of a strange boat. Lorna had never seen anything like her before. Her face, hair, even her clothes were covered in a dark red stain. She wore a badly sewn skraeling leather top and a wool skirt that was filthy and torn. But even from this distance, Lorna could make out a pair of unmistakable green eyes. They were the same eyes that had smiled at her since she was very small.

In her child's mind, she could easily explain the strange sight. Kiera had come back from the dead. Kiera had heard her daily prayers and now, thanks to her, Kiera's spirit was returning back to the village. By the colour of her reddened skin, it appeared that Lorna had rescued her friend from the eternal fires, which delighted her even more. She had managed to save her best friend from damnation. Her prayers to God had come true!

"Kiera!"

Lorna launched herself off the overhang and dropped into the river below.

*   *   *

Thorfinn saw Lorna a moment before she flung herself from the high riverbank.

"What is she thinking?" he cried as he watched her plummet into the river. "Come on, men! We have to get her out of the water before it's too late!"

As the warriors neared the embankment, they stopped in shock. The river's current was carrying little Lorna right into the path of a strange skraeling boat. It was bigger than the single-seated boats that had attacked the village in the earlier raids. It was strangely open-hulled, but there was no doubt that it was of a similar design. The two passengers inside the craft, however, nearly made his jaw drop. Red skraelings! The ghost people! And the one in the bow was female! Instinctively, he scanned for other attackers. Thankfully, he couldn't find any sign of a larger invasion. This might have been a peaceful encounter if it were not for that foolish child. Now he had no choice. He raised his spear and took aim at the lead skraeling. For Lorna's sake, he would have to kill them both.

But the female skraeling in the bow did

something completely unexpected. She stood up on her seat and threw herself off the boat into the water. She swam to Lorna, who immediately threw her arms around her in what seemed to be a happy embrace. Had the child completely lost her mind? They would have to take care of the female skraeling later. He readjusted his aim for the man in the rear of the craft. He hauled back his arm, then launched the spear.

*   *   *

If it hadn't been for the sun glinting off the sharpened iron point of the spear as it sailed over the water, Chocan would have been a dead man. With uncanny reflexes, he twisted his torso and shoulders. The spear skinned his chest and smacked heavily into the folded sail behind him, tearing through three layers of leather and coming to a stop just a hair from the skin hull.

Chocan quickly pulled the sail in front of him like a shield and leaned over the side of the boat.

"Kiera! They're attacking us!"

Kiera turned her head from Lorna's repeated kisses and looked back in horror at the large spear embedded in the sail. She spun to face the men on the riverbank.

"Don't attack! It's me! Kiera! We come in peace! Please, don't attack us!"

As Magnus and Gunnar were about to heave their own weapons at the craft, Thorfinn heard the pleas from the water. He held up a hand. The men froze. Thorfinn stared for a moment, his mind refusing to believe what he had just heard. A red skraeling speaking Nordic, claiming to be Kiera? But Kiera was dead! He had seen it with his own eyes. And yet, there was Lorna kissing and hugging this stranger.

"Kiera?" Thorfinn shouted, his voice revealing his confusion. "How can it be you?"

She laughed as the other red skraeling tentatively put the leather sail down. The strange craft pulled alongside the woman and child. The woman gently hoisted Lorna into the craft. Hanging on to the side of the inuak, Kiera beamed with excitement.

"It's a long story, perhaps worthy of a saga! I'll tell you all about it if you give us permission to paddle into the village."

Thorfinn's mind swirled. Lorna was sitting in a hated skraeling craft, kissing the stained woman on the top of her wet head. How was it possible? It had to be Keira!

"We will meet you at the dock," he replied, shaking his head in disbelief.

He turned to his men. They, too, were speechless, their weapons now lowered. Had they just witnessed a miracle? The shocked men ran back to the village. The incredible news spread like wildfire and every Viking in the entire village ran down to the dock to see for themselves the red skraeling slave girl who had somehow returned from the dead.

TWENTY-ONE

After disembarking and taking a moment to scrub the thick ochre from their skin, the exhausted travellers devoured a bowl of fish stew before attempting to answer the hundreds of questions being thrown at them by the disbelieving crowd. Finally, Keira stood up on a stump and raised her hands for silence. The villagers quieted in anticipation. Kiera wove the tale of her journey for her enraptured Viking audience. She described her daring swim to shore while caught in the heart of the fierce Atlantic storm. She then explained how she was captured by a bloodthirsty band of Beothuck warriors. They had dragged her in bonds back to their village, where they threw her in a darkened pit with only insects and rotten meat to eat for weeks on end. The Beothuck planned to sacrifice her to their gods of war when the first snow arrived. The Vikings muttered in fright at such a horrific situation, and Keira was pleased. She wanted the Vikings to fear the skraelings enough to hasten their departure.

She then explained how she had lost all hope until Chocan, one of the few caring Beothuck, had taken pity upon her. In the dead of night, he had rescued Kiera from her underground prison, and together they had escaped on foot through the endless forests. Always on the run, they were continuously hunted by the furious, revenge-seeking Beothuck. Still, they managed to scrape together meals during the cool autumn months by catching small game with traps and harvesting edible roots.

As winter approached, they had hiked northward through endless swamps that were home to terrifyingly huge predators, never before seen by European eyes. They were similar to the mythological creatures of Norse legend. There were human-like, slimy creatures who pulled their sleeping victims down into their underwater lairs, leaving only a trail of foul-smelling ooze as evidence of their capture. There were also huge swamp serpents whose venomous bite could kill a hundred men. Kiera also told of a cat-like animal which prowled the woods with foot-long fangs and cold, slitted eyes. The gathered crowd looked at each other in fear. Even the fighting men felt their throats dry as they absorbed the horrifying details.

To survive the dangerous conditions, Chocan and Kiera had huddled through the winter in a protective but damp cave. They had been too afraid to venture beyond the mouth of their shelter. They had almost starved to death during that terrible, dark season.

Finally, as spring approached and the snow began to melt, they had resumed their careful trek northward. Upon reaching the coast, they had stumbled onto a Thule camp. Kiera accurately described their capture, as well as their daring escape by sail in the stolen inuak. Then, on a serious note, Kiera emphasized to Thorfinn the news of the impending invasion. Over a hundred Thule warriors were out to seek revenge upon their village. The men looked at each other in concern while the women held on to their children with anxious dread.

Thorfinn shook his head in amazement. "You and Chocan did well to survive such an odyssey. We all thank you for alerting us to the impending attack. We were planning to leave for Greenland in a month, but because of your warning, I now challenge everyone to prepare for our departure in one week's time."

Whispers of disbelief rumbled throughout the crowd. One week felt like an impossible deadline. Thorfinn then turned to the newly-arrived travellers.

"Chocan, seeing that you can no longer return home to your skraeling tribe, you are welcome to stay with us. We could use an extra pair of strong hands around the village, that is, if you are willing to stay and help."

Kiera smiled. She translated Thorfinn's offer to Chocan. He paused, then replied in Beothuck. She nodded and turned back to Thorfinn.

"Chocan thanks you, and he accepts your generous offer."

The work started immediately. The crowd dispersed into their assigned groupings, each with an essential task to complete. Bedding, timber and roofing material for their future homes in Greenland were loaded on to the three docked longboats. The carpenters worked feverishly on the still-damaged fourth boat, knowing that if it didn't sail, important items for their future homes would have to remain behind. Kiera helped the women pack up the longhouses and repair the sails that would soon take them home.

Chocan contributed to the effort by helping to feed the famished workers. In an effort to preserve the livestock, Chocan offered to hunt and fish in the area surrounding the village. Each day he would return with loads of fresh fish and rabbit. Once he even managed to shoot and kill a large deer. The men of the village were stunned by the trapping and hunting skills of the newcomer.

Everyone was so busy that Chocan and Kiera could only find time to talk at dinner. Sitting at the main table in her family longhouse, Chocan was finally given an opportunity to feed his curiosity as well as his stomach. He asked Kiera about the strange animals that gave the villagers milk and eggs. He wanted to know the purpose of the wonderful metal objects that he had seen around the village. He asked about the people themselves and how they all tied into her previous tales of Nordic society. Chocan was most intrigued by Bjarni, the blacksmith. Chocan's fingertip rubbed the rusted head of a nail that helped secure the top of the table to the braces underneath.

"So he must be considered one of the most important men of the village."

"Yes," she agreed, digging her teeth into a leg of rabbit. "Without his skills, we would not be able to create and repair all of our metal objects."

"I would like to see his place of work, if that is permitted."

"Certainly. We could probably manage a visit tomorrow. But I don't know how much work you'll see. Bjarni is probably starting to pack away all of his equipment."

Kiera examined Chocan's face as his eyes roamed the noisy longhouse, his mind absorbing all of the sights, sounds and smells of the Viking culture. She suddenly realized how much he was really enjoying this time in her village. She lowered the meat she was eating and stared at her friend.

"I suppose there is no way to talk you into coming with us. You are certainly popular with the villagers."

Chocan reached over and took her hand. "The last few weeks have been incredible. I will never forget our journey together. But as you have your calling, so do I. My path lies with the Beothuck. No matter how tempting it is to possibly travel to the fabled land of the Teachers, I cannot abandon Nadie and my chosen people."

Kiera felt a lump grow in her throat. "I understand. It's just that I'm going to miss you so much."

Suddenly, a little head popped out from under the table. Lorna reached out a tiny hand and tapped Kiera on the shoulder.

"Are you two getting married?"

Kiera jumped, surprised by her sudden appearance.

"No, Lorna," she laughed. "We are not getting married."

They smiled at her innocence as Lorna's face dropped, but she turned and skipped back to her family.

184

"I told you," said Lorna's older sister. The entire table broke out in laughter.

Mats, sitting at the far end of the table, looked down at the strange Beothuck holding Kiera's hand and released a deep sigh of relief. He said a little prayer of thanks and reminded himself to do something special for Lorna the next time he had a chance. Now he knew that the skraeling would not be an obstacle.

Mats had been unable to take his eyes off Kiera since the day she had returned from the dead. Last year, he would have walked by her without giving her even a second glance. But now, everything about her had changed. Was it Kiera's newly found confidence, or her air of independent strength that he found so intoxicating? Her face seemed to glow. Or perhaps he had changed. His thoughts no longer dwelled constantly on the death of his first wife. As he reached for a second helping of fish, he made up his mind. He would meet with Bjorn and Dagmar after supper. It would be the required first step in order to seal their two destinies into one.

*   *   *

As the rising sun sliced through the early morning fog, Kiera stopped with Chocan at the entrance of the blacksmith's shop. Kiera was surprised to see Bjarni pumping the roaring bellows with his timber-sized arm. In his other hand, he held the end of a long handle that extended into the heart of the furnace. Attached to the end of the handle was a small metal cup. The heat from the furnace caused it to glow with an unearthly red pulse that was timed perfectly to the beating of the bellows.

"Hello, Bjarni!" shouted Kiera.

He glanced over his shoulder and smiled. "Well, if it isn't the immortal Irish girl herself. I've always heard you Irish were a lucky crew, but now I am a true believer. I see you've brought your friend along for a visit."

"Chocan wanted to see you at work. His people don't have metal objects."

He snorted. "It's a good thing, too. Imagine skraelings with metal weapons. It's the only advantage we have against them. If it wasn't for our metal, we'd have all been slaughtered by now."

"It's the Thule who attacked us, not the Beothuck," reminded Kiera.

Bjarni huffed. "What difference does it make? The picture you painted of the Beothuck a couple of days ago didn't exactly warm my heart to them either. They sound just as bad, if not worse, than the Thule."

Kiera frowned. She had momentarily forgotten about her tale. It was important for the Vikings to fear the Beothuck in order to keep them safe from future invasions. Perhaps she had embellished her tale too much.

"Well, they're not all like that. Chocan is proof. And there are others like him, too. Just not very many. In fact, the nice ones are like us in some ways...they are outnumbered, but somehow manage to hang on. The only difference being that they can't leave this land. We can."

Bjarni eyed Chocan suspiciously, who looked

back at him with a curious but friendly stare. "Except for Chocan, I've never met a skraeling that I could have liked. If there are more like him, then they have my sympathy."

Kiera turned to Chocan and explained Bjarni's activities. She told him that Bjarni was in the process of making nails. They watched as he heated the raw iron ore in the dish until it melted. Then he carefully poured the liquid into a row of narrow cone-shaped nail molds. After the red-hot liquid metal cooled to a hardened black, the nails were removed from the mold and Bjarni wielded a hammer to pound the nail into its final pointed shape. Finally, he picked up the nail with tongs and doused the finished product in water.

"Why is he making nails the day before you leave?" asked Chocan.

Kiera translated.

Bjarni laughed. "They ran out of nails for the last ship yesterday afternoon. Asked me to make up another handful. Sure, I told them, but you better not come crying for more nails tomorrow morning, because this is it. I'm through. I need tonight to organize my stuff for the voyage home. Nice place, this land. Love the trees. But I'd rather live in a village where the natives are more friendly."

Chocan smiled and thanked Bjarni in Nordic. Bjarni was impressed by the effort. "It should be me thanking you. Your warning of the invasion will save my family's life. If there's anything I can do for you, Chocan, you have only to ask," Keira translated.

Chocan scanned the room and noticed a pile of discarded items in the corner. Something near the bottom of the pile caught his eye. He walked over to a small, rectangular metal block and picked it up. It was another nail mold. He held it up.

"Is Bjarni throwing this out?" Kiera asked the blacksmith.

"What? That old mold?" snorted Bjarni. "Yeah, I was going to leave it here. The nails always come out crooked. Took too much time for me to straighten them out again with a hammer. He can have it if he wants it."

Kiera translated again, and Chocan thanked him. "One last thing, Kiera. Could you ask him if I could have a piece of his iron ore?"

Bjarni laughed. "Sure, take one. But only one. We had to lug our high grade ore all the way here from Scandinavia. Never did find a deposit of iron in Vinland that we could use."

As they left the blacksmith shop, Kiera looked at him suspiciously.

"What are you going to do?"

He grinned and held up the mold. "I've seen large amounts of this rock near Nadie's summer camp. Can you think of a better gift to give the Beothuck people?"

Kiera paused. She thought of all the implications that could follow by introducing iron to the Beothuck. She thought of the attacking Thule warriors and the possibility of the Vikings returning at a later time.

She returned the smile. "No, I can't."

TWENTY-TWO

In the early dawn of a new day, the loading was completed, and every villager had taken a position within the huge crafts. The village was only a shadow of its former self. The buildings had been stripped of their good timber and thatched roofs, the gardens and pastures were either harvested for future seeding or abandoned. The animals, removed from their comfortable village surroundings, bleated and clucked nervously in the centre of the longboats. The Vikings were nervous, sad and excited all at once. They couldn't stop gazing towards what had once been their picturesque home.

The captains shouted the order. The portside oars pushed against the log dock. The hulls of the four ships moved away in unison from the shore and out into the current of the river, moving slowly downstream and away from their abandoned village.

Kiera looked back from her position beside the mast. The ropes for hauling up the sail lay firmly in her hands. She was in the last of the four ships. A small craft bobbed along behind the stern of her boat. Chocan followed expressionlessly in the inuak, casually paddling in their wake. Kiera wondered what might be going through his mind. He had barely said a word to her all day. Before she had boarded the ship, they had hugged and said goodbye, but it had somehow felt incomplete and shallow. How does one say goodbye properly to a best friend and savior? His eyes were distant, but whatever he was thinking, he chose not to share it with Kiera. And she was afraid to ask.

Upon hearing that Chocan was choosing to stay in Vinland, the rest of the village was somewhat relieved. It would likely have caused grumblings among the Vikings in Greenland to have Chocan reside with them. Many had suffered attacks from Vinland skraelings in the past. Being new arrivals and in search of a home, they wouldn't want to make the transition to life in Greenland any more difficult than it had to be.

Kiera tore her eyes from Chocan and looked northward. What was the matter with her? If Chocan wanted to sulk at the moment of her departure, then that was his choice. For over a year, she had dreamed of this moment. She was standing on the deck of a Viking ship heading east! This was the first step in her long journey home.

As the ships rounded the last bend in the river, Kiera could feel the excitement welling up within her. There, beyond the far opening of the bay was the limitless horizon of ocean that would lead to Ireland.

A gentle nudge on her side snapped her out of her daydream. She was surprised to see Mats

190

standing next to her, looking off towards the ocean as well. The sea breeze ruffled his thick sandy hair as he leaned his broad shoulders against the side railing.

"I can see you're as excited as the rest of us. It actually feels good to finally leave this land."

The ocean wind whipped the curly hair that framed her smiling face.

"I've been waiting for this moment ever since we arrived," she replied.

He turned to her, squinting out the morning light. "I never had the chance to tell you how much the village changed after you became lost at sea. Without you, it was like the heart, the spark of the village had been stolen. But now that you're back, the entire village has come back to life. Your presence among us is such an important part of who we are."

Kiera shifted uneasily. She was getting an uncomfortable feeling about where this conversation might be going.

"Thank you, Mats, for your kind words. But one person cannot affect a whole village. It was probably just coincidence. The dark mood was more likely from the run of bad luck that struck the village in the past year. After all, I'm merely a slave girl."

"That can be changed."

Her eyes widened. "I'm sorry? What can be changed?"

"Perhaps you don't have to be a slave."

"I...I don't understand."

He took her hands in his. "I haven't stopped

thinking about you since you returned. You have touched my heart and my soul. I now realize that I don't want to live without you. I want you to be by my side, always. Kiera, I want you to marry me."

Her mouth dropped. "Marry you?"

"Yes! Marry me! You can be my wife, and with that distinction, you will no longer be considered a slave. You will be one of us!"

"But...but..." stammered Kiera, "what about Dagmar and Bjorn? They would have to agree to this!"

Frantically, her eyes scanned the boat. Sitting on a wooden bench, just behind the bow, she caught the beaming faces of Dagmar and Bjorn, their heads nodding up and down. Lorna, on all fours and talking to a crated chicken, was oblivious to the drama taking place. Kiera was astounded. They had already arranged this marriage amongst themselves!

"I can tell you're shocked," chuckled Mats. "We thought it would be fun to surprise you with the terrific news. And what a great day to propose! It's the first day of our new life away from Vinland. So, what do think?"

Marriage! Kiera's mind spun wildly from all of the implications. If she married Mats, they would live in Greenland for the rest of her life. She would no doubt be bearing children as soon as possible to help out with the backbreaking labour of living in such a marginal land. Marriage and children would tie her to the Vikings and this community forever. Her dream of Ireland suddenly faded to black. They had won. The Vikings had forcefully taken her from her homeland, and they would now trap her and all of her descendants among their people forever.

It was hard to believe that this was a scenario she had contemplated, even wished for, not so long ago. What had happened to her? Did it matter? There was no choice. It was extremely rare for a Viking to find a slave girl worthy of marriage. It was a huge honour for Kiera, one that she dared not refuse. To do so would be an insult to the entire community. She turned to Mats. Her lips parted to deliver her answer.

"Skraelings!"

Their hands broke apart. Mats and Kiera wheeled around, staring in horror to the northeast. The word that sent shivers down the spine of every villager was echoing from boat to boat. Fingers pointed to the north. A fleet of fast-moving kayaks materialized from behind the rocky northern tip of the bay, heading towards the river's mouth. The lead kayak spied the emerging Viking ships. The entire fleet of smaller kayaks changed heading. They began to paddle south. At once, Kiera realized what they were trying to do. She turned to Thorfinn, who was manning the rudder.

"They're trying to cut us off from the ocean!"

"Aye," he shouted back. "And we can't fight. Not with the women and children on board. It will have to be a race for the open sea. Well, Kiera, it is time to see what your repaired sails can do. Hoist them up! Let's make a run for it!"

Kiera and Mats heaved on the lines. The sail skidded up the mast, filling with a warm southwest wind. After several shouts between the captains, the other boats followed suit. The villagers fell into an anxious silence, their eyes staring at the approaching kayaks and their narrowing escape route. Every Viking knew that it would be close. Some closed their eyes in prayer. Some encouraged the wind to blow with greater force. Everyone had forgotten about the tiny inuak paddling along behind the massive longboats. Everyone, that was, except Kiera.

She leaned over the side of the boat and worriedly looked back. Chocan was paddling furiously, trying his best to keep up with the accelerating longboats. She knew that there was no way the Thule had missed seeing him as well. From personal experience, she knew the Thule loved revenge. Kiera cringed while thinking of what they might do to an escaped prisoner in a stolen Thule craft.

Chocan was slowly falling behind. She glanced forward towards the kayaks. Chocan was not going to make it. Kiera left the mast, ran towards the rear of the boat and took a long coil of rope from the deck. She lashed the end of the rope to the gunwale and took the heavy coil in her arms. Thorfinn, hands glued to the tiller beside her, stared at her incredulously.

"What do you think you're doing?"

"I'm getting this rope to Chocan. If we don't pull him beyond the reach of the Thule, he'll be killed."

Thorfinn looked over his shoulder at the tiny craft. He shook his head sadly.

"I'm sorry, Kiera. You'll never be able to throw the rope that far."

She threw the coil onto her shoulder. "Who said anything about throwing?"

In one swift motion, she grabbed Thorfinn's knife from his belt then threw herself over the side of the boat.

"Kiera!"

The icy water hit her like a wall. Her ribs took the brunt of the impact, crushing the air from her lungs. Fighting the urge to breathe, she released the coil, except for the very end, stuck the knife between her teeth and quickly tied the rope around her waist. Then, with every last ounce of strength, she tore at the water with her arms and legs. She willed herself upwards, fighting against the weight of the rope and the screaming in her lungs.

After what seemed like an eternity, her head finally broke the surface. She gasped, filling her burning lungs with life-giving air. Where was he? She spun, disoriented. There! Amazingly, the inuak was almost upon her. Chocan tossed the paddle into the inuak and desperately leaned over the side. Kiera's eyes were wide with fear as the weight of the rope began to pull her back under. Chocan speared his hand through the surface and grabbed her by the back of her coat. He heaved. Her head broke the surface and with two hands, he grabbed her under her armpits.

Coughing, she wrapped her arms around his shoulders, but at the same moment, the rope snapped taut. Kiera screamed as her body felt it had just been ripped in two. The knife that was in her mouth clattered onto the rib below. Chocan gabbed hold of the rope, preventing her from being thrown back into the sea, then he held on. He picked up the knife which lay by his knee and slashed it down upon the rope that stretched away from Kiera's waist. Bracing his foot against the ribbing, he tied the rope to the forward thwart. He slowly relaxed the muscles in his arms, allowing the boat to absorb the tension. Miraculously, the thwart held. The inuak skipped through the waves as it followed Thorfinn's longboat. He turned his attention to Kiera, who lay groaning at his feet.

"You crazy woman!" he shouted. "What did you think you were doing?"

Kiera turned to the side and retched out a lungful of sea water. She looked up through bloodshot eyes.

"I was trying to save your life," she gurgled.

"By killing yourself?" he yelled, furiously.

She blinked into the bright sun. "The Thule would have caught you. I couldn't let that happen."

His tone softened. He gently touched the bruise which showed at her exposed waist. She yelped as he pushed gently on her side.

"I think you might have cracked a couple of your ribs. Try to lie still. I'm afraid that we are not out of danger yet."

"Why?"

"Your friend Thorfinn just saved your life. You would have drowned if he had not ordered down the sail. Otherwise you would have been pulled under before I could have reached you. His effort, however, might just cost us all. Although we're sailing once again, Thorfinn's delay has allowed the Thule to close the gap to the ocean."

Despite the fiery pain from her ribs, Kiera rolled onto her hands and knees and looked forward. The Viking ship was plowing impressively through the water, dragging the insignificant inuak in its wake. Thorfinn looked over his shoulder at the tiny craft, his face lined with concern. Kiera waved. Thorfinn nodded grimly, then returned to navigating the ship through the ever narrowing gap between the land and the kayaks. The first three ships were now well ahead and already sailing safely into the open ocean.

The Thule were so close that their furious faces could be seen. They knew that they were not going to catch the fourth and final ship. Their focus shifted to the tiny inuak. Perhaps their wrath could be taken out upon the two passengers in tow. The Thule raised their arrows and took aim. Thorfinn signalled for everyone on board the longboat to duck. Kiera and Chocan dove under the leather. She yelped as arrows began smacking into their protective shield like a hailstorm. One arrow did manage to slice through the leather. Kiera flinched as it grazed her shoulder.

Miraculously, the slaps of incoming arrows began to dissipate. It wasn't until the ocean could be heard lapping against the bow that Kiera peered out carefully from under her cover and surveyed the surrounding scene. The flotilla of kayaks sat motionless behind them in the mouth of the bay. The Thule looked on helplessly as their prey escaped, disappearing into the ocean beyond the mouth of the bay.

"Hold tight!" shouted Thorfinn, as the sail was

lowered once again. "I'll pull you alongside."

Kiera and Chocan came out from under the sail. She stiffened as she saw the blood oozing once again from his injured back.

"Your shoulder!"

"It must have been from the paddling," he answered, grimacing as he gingerly tried to move it up and down.

Thorfinn looked over the railing at the inuak. At least two dozen arrows were embedded in every part of the craft. He shook his head, wondering how anyone could have survived the assault.

"Are you two all right?" he shouted doubtfully.

"Chocan hurt his shoulder again," she shouted back, taking a cloth. She soaked it in sea water, then wrapped it around his injured back.

"If he's hurt, then we'd better bring him along to Greenland after all. He won't be able to paddle back to land in that condition."

"You're right," said Kiera as they bobbed alongside. "I don't think he will be able to paddle back, either."

"Then let's get going," Thorfinn said, lowering his hand over the side. "We have to catch up to the other ships before nightfall."

Kiera looked into Thorfinn's weathered face and shook her head. "I'm not going with you."

Thorfinn's eyes widened in shock. "What?"

"I'm going to take Chocan back home."

"But he no longer has a home!"

She looked back at Chocan, then up at Thorfinn with a calm, knowing gaze. "You're wrong, Thorfinn. He does. And I think I just realized that it is my home as well."

Mats appeared at Thorfinn's side.

"Kiera! What are you doing?"

She smiled warmly at the confused young Viking. "Mats, I like you, but there is no way I'm going to marry you. Sorry."

Kiera swung the knife and severed the line between herself and the Vikings. She watched placidly as the longboat pulled away. The stunned faces of the Viking crew melted into the hazy morning mist.

"What are you doing?" asked Chocan.

He was just as shocked as the Vikings by the turn of events. She gazed towards the fading ship, watching in silence as the vessel and ocean became one. Then, slowly, she turned to gaze into his bewildered eyes. She reached out and touched him on the arm.

"You were right all along, Chocan. Going home to Ireland was just a dream. I know now that I have already found my home and family. It has been right here all along."

Picking up the paddle, she turned the inuak south. Choosing her distant landmark, Kiera rode the waves back towards the rugged but welcoming coast.

TWENTY-THREE

One Year Later

The caribou hunt was once again a success. The entire Beothuck nation celebrated their good fortune with several planned days of joyous festivity. On the first night, after the massive feast but before the raucous dancing was to begin, Chocan stood up behind the crude table laden with cooked delicacies and raised his arms for attention. The table itself was a topic of wondrous discussion, for the legs were braced with strange sharp stones that Kiera and Chocan called nails.

Chocan waited for the large crowd to calm, then he went on once again to describe the adventures he and Kiera had shared on their way to the Viking village. The tale of their escape from the Thule was met with awe and excitement. Howls of laughter erupted as Chocan described how Kiera had spun stories of evil monsters and nasty bands of Beothuck, all prepared to destroy any future Viking incursion. It was a shock to everyone when Chocan, at the end of his story, announced that he and Kiera would be leaving.

"Why?" asked Nadie, the first to recover from the news.

Chocan nodded to Kiera, who stood up and moved to his side.

"I want to take Kiera for a visit to the village of the Teachers. To my home. Since she will never be able to return to Ireland, she should at least see what her ancestors were able to accomplish here, across the ocean from her homeland. Sooleawaa has agreed to stay with you and continue the Teaching."

"When will you return?"

"We don't know."

"And when will you leave?"

"As soon as possible. To take advantage of the northern winds but before the winter storms begin to blow."

Nadie frowned. She stood up and gathered with the other elders. While the elders conversed, Shawnadit ran up from the outer tables and wrapped herself around Kiera. Kiera couldn't believe how much her little angel had grown in only a year. The skirt Shawnadit was wearing and had created with her own needle was an excellent first effort for the young seamstress.

"You're leaving again?" asked Shawnadit, upset at the news.

Kiera lowered herself to one knee and lifted the young girl's fallen chin with her finger.

"Yes, but I will come back. Chocan is taking me on a trip to see his home."

Shawnadit squeezed her. "Can I please come too?"

"I would love to take you, my little shadow, but it will be a very dangerous ocean crossing. I'm not going to risk your life out on the open ocean."

"I don't mind," Shawnadit said hopefully.

"But I do," replied Kiera. "You have to look after Nadie and the rest of the band for me. Your skirt is the talk of the Meeting Place. You'll be in charge of garment repairs while I am away."

Shawnadit nodded solemnly, then enveloped Kiera in an enormous hug.

"Hurry back."

The young girl ran back to her table as the elders returned.

"We have decided that we would like to help you in any way possible. The trip is long and dangerous. In our lives, no one has attempted a crossing from east to west."

Chocan stepped forward. "Thank you, Nadie, and thank you to the other elders as well. I know the trip west will have its risks, but we are willing to accept those risks. I am sorry that I must leave you for a short time. You are my family, and we promise to return."

"You are my family as well," offered Kiera. "I will never be able to thank you enough for adopting me into your tribe and into your hearts."

Nadie nodded. "Kiera, you are as much a daughter to me as any other member of my band. Thank you for choosing us as your family. And Chocan, I speak for the entire nation when I say that we will miss you. You have brought a great amount of joy and prosperity to our people. May you and Kiera have a safe trip home."

"We are going back to my place of birth," said Chocan, pausing, "but here, with you, will always be my home."

TWENTY-FOUR

The massive sea canoe was portaged in shifts by six muscular warriors through the descending hills of the western woods. Chocan and Kiera were glad for the help. They already had their hands full with their own bags and belongings. It took nearly a week for the group to reach their destination. It was the only southwestward flowing river in this part of Beothuck territory. Chocan thanked the warriors for their help by presenting them with a surprise. He passed to each one a carefully crafted harpoon tip, copied from the one he had discovered in the Thule inuak. The warriors, stone-faced and mainly silent for the entire journey, lit up with childish excitement. They couldn't believe that they finally had this long-sought prize in their hands. Chocan carefully explained how the weapon worked, then wished them luck with the spring seal hunt. The ecstatic warriors thanked the two travellers before heading back to the Meeting Place with smiles that could have brightened the entire night sky.

The next day, Kiera took the bow, while Chocan manned the stern of the canoe. Chocan concentrated on the steering of the craft down the tricky river. He needed to be careful, for their canoe was designed with a deep, pointed keel that, in the ocean, would provide them with stability, but could be easily damaged on shallow boulders.

It took a week for them to reach the salt water of the ocean. They followed the craggy shore until they came to a narrow peninsula that stretched out towards the western ocean, set aflame by the setting crimson sun.

Chocan guided the canoe into a protected cove, where they unloaded the craft, then pulled it safely away from the water's edge. The nearby clearing would be their temporary home.

"This is where I met my first Beothuck many years ago," he explained as he led the hike up the rocky face of the cliff to a ledge that looked majestically over the seemingly unending expanse of ocean. He pointed just south of where the sun had set only moments before.

"There. That is Mi'kmaq territory."

Kiera squinted at the hazy line, where the crimson sky met the sea.

"I don't see anything but water. Are you sure?" asked Kiera.

Chocan smiled. "You doubt me? Only on a perfect day can a smudge of land been seen on the horizon. But trust me, it is there."

"What do we do now?" asked Kiera.

"We wait."

"Wait for what?"

"Wait for the wind to be just right. With the help of your leather cloud, it should be a two-day journey.

This is a dangerous time of year to attempt the crossing. Fierce windstorms can strike with little warning. We must be careful in determining which night will be best for the attempt."

"Night?" questioned Kiera. "Would it not be easier paddling in the day?"

He shook his head. "At night, the wind calms, and the waves will not be as threatening. It will be safer travelling then."

"So we might be here for a while."

Chocan nodded. "We will have to be patient but ready to go at a moment's notice."

Kiera reached forward and playfully smudged the ochre on Chocan's cheek. "So do your people stain themselves as well?"

Chocan smiled. "It has been so long that I had nearly forgotten. No, they do not. We'll have to scrub ourselves clean before we leave."

Kiera laughed. "We better set up camp. I'll go and get our blankets."

Kiera disappeared down the path that led back to the clearing. Chocan turned as well, but hesitated. His eyes were drawn back to the western twilight. After all of their adventures in the past year, was he now pushing their luck with this final journey? Did he dare take Kiera out into the middle of the ocean on a voyage that had not been attempted in more than a generation?

He took a deep breath. Then a voice echoed in his mind... Important decisions should be made with your heart and your mind. He said a prayer, reached into his soul, and listened. The reply came as a whisper in the wind. His worries and fears gently evaporated. Smiling, he turned and started down the path after Kiera.

*   *   *

It was five days before the weather chose to cooperate with the travellers. From the north came a gentle but chilly breeze. The pounding waves that had been crashing against the mighty cliffs calmed to a gentle rumble. The adventurers were ready. With the canoe packed, they pushed off with the morning breeze and paddled westward. The craft bobbed on the open ocean as Kiera lifted the sail into position. The deep keel of the canoe kept the tiny ocean craft on course as she manned the sails and Chocan worked his paddle in a rudder-like fashion.

As midnight approached, the wind that had been so helpful completely dissipated, and they had to resort to using their paddles in order to continue their westward journey. A sea of twinkling stars filled the ebony sky above their heads. Chocan guided the craft towards a star in the west. As it was about to disappear, he chose the next star above it as their guiding light.

"With the ocean this calm," commented Chocan, "we should be able to make Tuywegannmikuk by daybreak."

"Where?" asked Kiera, muffling a yawn with the back of her hand.

"It's a small island between our two lands. It will give us shelter in case the weather changes."

"I can't believe that there's no wind tonight. I don't think I've ever seen the ocean this calm before."

"Nor I," agreed Chocan, concern in his voice.

"Are you worried about something?" asked Kiera.

"Yes. Look ahead."

Kiera strained her eyes to see what was bothering Chocan, but all she could see was inky darkness.

"I don't see anything."

"Exactly. Where are the stars?"

She looked again, and a chill ran down her spine. Along the horizon, the stars had disappeared, replaced by a band of forbidding black.

"What is it?"

Chocan paused. "Fog."

A light mist began to tickle Kiera's face as they continued to plow westward with renewed enthusiasm. Within minutes, however, the fog had erased almost the entire sky. They both stopped paddling.

"I've lost the star," said Chocan, concern in his voice. "Without it, we might end up paddling our canoe in circles."

Kiera's mind swirled, trying to think of a solution to their dilemma. An idea pulled her eyes upwards.

"It's all right," said Kiera, calmly. "We can still use the stars."

"How?" asked Chocan. "We have no idea which way is west."

"My Viking masters made up stories to go along with each pattern, or constellation, of stars," she explained. "And these patterns are fixed in the sky, always in the same orientation, moving east to west. I recognize that group up there," she said, pointing up and to the right, "the one that looks like a big plow; it is always north. So if we keep it to our right, then we will still be heading west."

"Good," said Chocan, looking at the constellation to which she was pointing. "Just one thing, Kiera. What's a plow?"

Kiera giggled. "It's a thing that's dragged behind a horse for planting... Wait, you don't know what a horse is, either. You know what? Why don't we switch places and you let me steer. After a year of watching you crash us into rocks and shoals, I think I can now handle the stern seat."

"The stern is yours," offered Chocan, laughing.

After a moment of shuffling around the stored baggage, they set off again, heading into the cool mist. They paddled until the sky began to brighten with the anticipated sunrise. The fog, however, thickened above them until even the stars above had disappeared.

They stopped once again.

"Now what? The stars are completely gone. And I don't think the fog is going to let us see the sunrise either."

Chocan held up his hand.

"Do you hear it?" he whispered.

Kiera paused. "What?"

"Listen."

Beyond the lapping of the waves against the hull was what sounded like the deep snores of a huge animal. The rumbling disappeared, only to occur once more. It continued in a slow, rhythmic pattern. Chocan smiled. "The island."

Using the sound of the breakers to guide them,

the paddlers pushed forward, stopping every so often to discuss the direction of the sound. In a surprisingly short amount of time, the distant roar developed into a colossal boom. The waves started to increase in size.

"I think we're close," said Chocan.

Suddenly, a towering rocky cliff materialized out of the grey gloom directly in front of them. A wave grabbed the canoe and launched it towards the jagged teeth of the thundering rock face.

"I think we're too close!" shouted Kiera.

In panic, Kiera and Chocan paddled ferociously backwards against the foaming breakers. Sea water crashed over the stern, soaking not only their backs but all of their belongings as well. They were wet and shivering by the time they eased their way back into the rolling waves of the open ocean. Keeping a safe distance from the ominous shore, Chocan steered them around to the opposite end of the island, where the sheer cliffs gave way to a small, protective harbour.

Thankfully, they pulled the canoe out of the ocean and onto a pebbled beach. Unloading their belongings, the two retreated away from the shore and built a simple shelter under the protection of a small cave within the foot of a towering slab of rock. Chocan and Kiera crawled underneath their damp blankets and fell sound asleep.

It was afternoon before they awoke to the cries of seagulls and the light of the afternoon sun. Kiera rubbed her sore shoulders.

"My shoulders are as tight as knots," commented Kiera. "How are yours?"

Chocan rubbed his middle. "I don't think there is an ache in my body that compares to the rumbling in my stomach."

Kiera laughed. "I can take a hint. You get the fire going, and I'll prepare dinner."

Night was already falling by the time they sat on their driftwood benches and sipped on a delicious seafood soup, followed by dried berries. Chocan looked out at the sky beyond the breakers on the beach.

"The wind is still calm. We may be able to continue the journey to my home tonight."

Kiera could see the excitement in his eyes. "That's fantastic news. From what I saw this morning, I think the less time we spend on this desolate island, the better. How can I help?"

Chocan picked up a dry piece of driftwood.

"We need to gather as much wood as possible."

"But we already have enough for cooking our dinner," she pointed out.

"Not for cooking, for a signal," he explained. "We will start a bonfire here on the beach. If all goes well, we will see a response from my nation tonight."

After an hour of gathering and piling, several burning sticks from the cooking fire were brought to a towering pile of driftwood near the water's edge. It didn't take long for the ocean breeze to whip the wood into a raging bonfire. Sparks danced high into the darkening sky. They sat on a large piece of west-facing driftwood and told stories of the sea until the full moon rose high into the night sky.

"There!" she yelled, pointing into the darkness.

Where the land had melted into the inky black of night, a tiny spot of orange could be seen, flickering like the tiniest of fireflies.

Chocan rose and stepped towards the already packed canoe. "Let's go."

Using the sail and favourable winds, the coast of the distant land slowly approached, until the sound of booming breakers welcomed the travellers to their final destination. Chocan guided them along the coast towards the light of the fire. In the morning twilight, he spied a small beach. He turned the canoe towards the shore and expertly rode a breaker up onto the sandy landing. They dragged the canoe to the edge of a pine forest, scraped together a rough mattress of needles, and threw their blankets on top of the pile. It was midday before Kiera managed to rouse herself for breakfast.

Chocan had a meal of cooked fish already prepared. Although their bodies were sore from two days of paddling, they agreed to continue the voyage. They sailed southwest, along the base of breathtaking rocky cliffs that were capped with vast expanses of green forests. Chocan explained that the fire had been on the top of one of the cliffs. Kiera, however, could not find any sign of human activity. Eventually, the cliffs gave way to magnificent forests that stretched right down to the ocean's rocky shore. It was early evening when they rounded a point that opened up into a deep bay. Kiera pointed to the first sign of human life in this new land. A thin column of black smoke rose up from behind the wind-swept cedars at the far end of the bay.

There they found a dozen empty canoes lining the muddy shore of a river. They were different from the Beothuck design, with flatter bottoms and no rise midway along their sides. Chocan ran their canoe up next to the others. Kiera jumped over the side and dragged the bow up onto the mud.

A twig snapped behind her. Surprised, she spun and looked into the handsome face of a tall man with a long, hawkish nose. His hair was long, braided and light brown. He wore an open vest and a pair of dyed leather pants. His almond-coloured eyes seemed transfixed by her friendly green-eyed stare. Kiera stepped forward, her hand extended.

"Good evening," she said in Celtic. "My name is Kiera."

The man's mouth gaped open in surprise. He tried to respond, but the words were caught in his throat. He wheeled around and ran into the woods, yelling at the top of his lungs in a language that Kiera didn't understand. Chocan, now at her side, laughed.

Kiera shook her head. "I don't know why I have that effect on people when I first meet them."

"Come on. Let me show you my village."

Together, they followed a short path through the woods that ended at a large clearing. Kiera stopped in her tracks and gasped. Memories and images from her childhood flooded back into her mind. There, in full glory, was an almost exact replica of her Irish village, complete with a protective, picketed fence. In the centre of the village stood a magnificent stone church, complete with a huge wooden cross and sod roof.

An Irish stone building! Just the sight of it alone brought tears to her eyes. Kiera surveyed the rest of the village in disbelief. A central wooden tower, similar to the ones she had seen in Ireland, rose up from behind the church, giving scouts a view of both the forest and bay. Tiny sod huts were clustered together to the west side of the village like a group of oversized anthills.

On the east side of the village stood a more typical native settlement. Longhouses lined the inside of the protective fence. There was also a large outdoor meeting area, a cooking shelter and racks for the drying of skins. Word of the newly-arrived strangers spread like wildfire throughout the community. People poured out of the longhouses and woods, gathering at the village entrance in a silent mass. As they approached the gate, Kiera studied the sea of curious faces. Their open eyes and slightly wider cheekbones quietly echoed their common ancestry.

The crowd parted, allowing them passage through the gate and into the village. An older man materialized from the crowd and stood before them. Kiera and Chocan came to a halt while he examined them thoroughly. Chocan stepped forward, lowered himself onto one knee and kissed the leader's right hand. The older man put his weathered hands on either side of Chocan's face and gently brought him back up onto his feet. Kiera could sense something more than just recognition as they stared at each other in silence. Finally, Chocan leaned forward, wrapping his arms around the fragile shoulders of the older man.

"Father!"

The elder embraced his son. "How are you, Chocan?"

"Very well, father."

They pulled away from each other. Chocan's father turned to face Kiera.

"And who have we here?"

"Father," Chocan said, proudly, "I would like to introduce you to my friend, Kiera. Kiera, this is Niskamij, my father."

Kiera looked down humbly, knelt and greeted Chocan's father in the same fashion.

"Thank you for allowing me to visit your wonderful home," she said in Celtic.

"Ah, the tongue of the Teachers," Niskamij said, his brow wrinkling in recognition. "You have indeed travelled a long way. This is certainly a cause for celebration. Welcome to our village, Kiera. There is so much for us to talk about."

Chocan placed a gentle hand on Kiera's back. She looked up into his eyes. There was more than excitement in his gaze. His hand slid down to her arm and gently took her hand in his. Kiera returned the smile in a way that Chocan had only dreamed he would some day see. At that very moment, their spirits entwined and became one. She squeezed his hand. Her voice could simply not find the words.

He tilted his head toward the village.

"Let me show you around."

Chocan led her forward. Close behind followed the dozens of villagers, chattering among themselves about what all of this could possibly mean. Niskamij guided them towards the cooking area. The aroma of a dinnertime meal tickled the senses of the hungry travellers. But as they passed through the centre of the settlement, Kiera came to a stop.

The huge cross that she had seen from a distance was beautifully carved with traditional geometric Celtic patterns. Kiera took the cross that hung around her neck and gently rubbed it between her finger and thumb. She allowed the image of the cross that dominated her vision to sear itself into her memory. Savouring the moment, she closed her eyes, took a deep breath and smiled. Her soul, for the first time since she was a little girl, was at peace. She was home.

EPILOGUE

July 12th, 1604
Southeast shore of Cape Breton Island
"Over there?"

Stunned, Samuel de Champlain pointed to the far shore of the bay.

The old chief nodded.

Samuel could not take his eyes off the stone that hung around the chief's neck. It was an intricately carved Celtic cross. It was impossible that the Irish had recently arrived here in these lands. Ireland was the poorest, most backwards-thinking country in all of Europe. They didn't have one vessel capable of making this journey across the Atlantic. Yet, here was this native chief with a piece of classic Celtic adornment.

Although Samuel had been hired by Commander De Chaste to map the recently claimed French coastline, Samuel himself could not resist a good mystery. Ever since he was a child, he had dreamed of one day making a discovery that would make him famous. He had already travelled with his father to the fabled city of the Aztecs called Mexico in the far south of this New World. He was stunned by the wealth and riches that had been acquired by the Spanish through the pillaging of both the Aztec and Inca lands. He wondered whether this northern wilderness might hold a similar find of history-changing proportions. A Celtic cross on the wrong side of an ocean was certainly an intriguing clue to a mystery.

After several more hand gestures and a bag of glass beads, Samuel convinced the chief to loan him two of his Mi'kmaq warriors and a canoe so that he might investigate the area to which the chief had pointed. He turned to a young French officer, who was overseeing the loading of wooden casks filled with fresh drinking water. One skiff was already rowing its way back to the majestic three-masted ship that lay anchored further out in the deeper water of the bay.

"Oh, come on, Henri," Samuel teased, shoving his friend. "I know you have an ounce of adventure somewhere in that officer's uniform. Let's go find out what these natives are hiding on the other side of the bay."

Henri shook his head. "No way, Samuel. If I leave my post, De Chaste will have me tied to the mast and lashed. You're not an officer of the French navy. If you want to take off with these savages and have a knife put in your back when you're not looking, that's up to you. Just don't expect us to drag your stinking hide all the way back to France. If you die here, then De Chaste will bury you here."

Samuel shook his head, smiling. "I just don't understand you, Henri. You travel all the way across the ocean to this magnificent, unexplored world and you're still happiest when you have locked yourself away in your cabin. How can you possibly choose reading over a true adventure?"

"To each his own," rebuked Henri.

Samuel started for the canoe. "I'll return shortly."

"God be with you," Henri quietly muttered to his friend, then turned his attention back to his crew. "Come on! Put your backs into it! We have to get these casks filled and returned to the ship before sundown!"

*   *   *

Samuel helped push the canoe into the water, then climbed aboard between the two lean warriors. He took in a deep breath of the fresh summer air as the canoe slid through the water towards the far shore of the bay. He couldn't help but smile. Truly, he didn't care if all he found were simply more trees and rocks. It was invigorating to finally be by himself, far away from the ship that had held him captive for almost four months.

He allowed his thoughts to wander into the future. The King was paying him handsomely to map out the best locations for future villages in this massive territory. Using his imagination, Samuel could see French fishing boats plying the water with their bountiful catches, children playing under the wharfs along the shoreline and the smell of homemade bread drifting across the still water. Yes, New France would soon be a sight to behold. He felt honoured to be playing a key role in its nurturing and birth.

The canoe slid to a stop in the soft mud. The silent warriors held the canoe while Samuel stepped out, almost losing his balance on the slippery surface. Safely on firm ground, he waited for the warriors to store their paddles and join him on shore. They led him along a well-worn path into the woods. After a two minute jaunt, the trees suddenly opened up into a partial clearing. A green mound rose up from the centre of the clearing, while smaller, less prominent mounds were scattered around the periphery. Younger trees were flourishing throughout the area, their branches stretching out to the life-giving rays of the bright afternoon sun. Samuel could gauge roughly by the age of the trees that the clearing had been deserted for at least several decades. Even worse, there was nothing here that pointed towards the possibility of treasure. The area was quite unremarkable.

Then, to his surprise, the two warriors turned to the right, fell onto their knees and made the sign of the cross on their chest. After that, they lowered themselves until they were prostrate with the forest floor.

The sign of the cross? How could they possibly know that? But then what about the Celtic cross of their chief? Perhaps this area did require further examination.

He left the warriors and stepped forward. Something snagged his foot, and he fell hard onto his hands. He looked down and discovered that his feet had become entangled within a collapsed heap of long, rotting branches. Some of the branches were still bound together, as if they had been part of a fence at one time. Moving more carefully, weaving in and out of the young saplings, Samuel worked his way towards the centre of the clearing. On either side he noticed the distinct mounds. Something bothered him about the symmetry of the whole area. He had seen it before, from one of the hundreds of maps he had studied over the years. The answer was frustratingly beyond his reach.

When he arrived at the centre of the clearing, he began to climb the hill, but stopped again when his ankle slipped into a rocky fissure. The small hill was actually a pile of stones. Some were still fitted together as if they were once part of a building. He had yet to see any evidence of stone buildings in this new land. The mystery deepened.

He began to search around the hill for more clues. His foot hit something solid. Bending over, he pulled at a mat of vines until the object was partially revealed. It was a large, carved piece of wood, roughly the size of a ship's beam. He continued to remove the creepers and weeds, following the beam until it intersected with a second larger piece of wood. He froze. It couldn't be...

Samuel, his hands trembling, quickly finished the excavation. Fully uncovered, he stood back in awe, stunned at the enormity of his discovery. The pile of stones, the symmetrical mounds and the natives crossing themselves at the edge of the clearing all suddenly made sense. He now knew exactly what this place used to be.

His jaw dropped even further as he looked off to

the far edge of the clearing. In the direction of the warriors stood a small field filled with row upon row of small wooden crosses. Some were so old that they lay sprawled on the ground, decomposing. Others, however, were upright and very recently constructed. A graveyard that was still in use! No wonder the warriors had bowed in respect.

Samuel ran. The natives, surprised to see him fly down the path, took chase after him. By the time they had caught up, Samuel had already pushed the canoe back into the water. He was wildly signalling for the warriors to paddle him directly to the anchored ship.

*   *   *

In the confines of Commander De Chaste's private cabin, Samuel breathlessly explained to him what he had found. De Chaste, considered one of The King's most loyal commanders and awarded accordingly, sat behind his mahogany desk, his narrow eyes sizing up the young mapmaker.

Samuel shifted uncomfortably. The commander was as cool as ever, but still, Samuel could sense something was wrong.

"Does anyone else know of this discovery?" asked De Chaste.

Samuel shook his head. "No, sir. I came straight to you."

"That makes it much easier," De Chaste muttered to himself.

"Makes what easier, sir?" asked Samuel, confused.

De Chaste leaned forward and stared at

Samuel with a gaze that could wither the most hardy plant.

"You are to tell no one about your discovery."

"Tell no one? I don't understand, sir."

The commander leaned back in his chair. "I want to see this place for myself. Are those savages still on board?"

"I believe so. But sir, I..."

"Then we will leave immediately. They will take us. Go make the arrangements."

* * *

As Samuel de Champlain led Commander De Chaste up the path to the clearing, he was confused by his commander's coolness to the discovery. He had not asked a single question during the canoe trip. Even more surprising was the commander's strict order of secrecy.

Surely, thought Samuel, seeing the sight will change his attitude. As they broke into the clearing, the two warriors once again crossed themselves and fell face down onto the ground. The commander was unmoved by their actions and simply stepped over the savages. Samuel led the tour.

"It is definitely a village built on the Irish design, sir. These tangled pieces of wood used to be a stockade-style defensive wall. The wood itself is no longer bound together, but you can still make out the circular shape. We just passed through what would have been the gate to the village and this pathway led down to the village centre. Over there, those long mounds would have been the living quarters for the families of the village. And I think that pile of rotting wood may be what is left of a watch tower."

"I've been to Ireland," commented De Chaste finally, and much to Samuel's relief. "Their villages look nothing like what you are describing here."

"Ah, perhaps not now," explained Samuel, "but I have studied the designs of villages built hundreds of years ago. This village has exactly the similar dimensions and structures as those earlier Irish settlements. I am guessing this village is based on a design that was used between 700 and 1000 A.D."

De Chaste snorted. "I find this all hard to believe."

Samuel smiled. "Wait until you see what lies in the centre of the village."

Samuel led the commander to the rotten, but enormous uncovered cross. Samuel beamed with pride as if he had found the treasure of King Solomon. De Chaste looked down at the cross, then scanned the entire village area with a cold, calculating gaze.

"Is this it?" he asked.

Samuel's face dropped. "Uh...yes, sir. Isn't the cross magnificent? And these stones behind me are what I think must have been a church. Commander, we have just discovered an Irish settlement that is likely hundreds of years old! It is an incredible find! Who would have thought those primitive Celts could have travelled so far in their skin-covered boats?"

De Chaste turned to Samuel, his face warming ever so slightly. "Samuel, you have discovered nothing. This is simply a series of dirt mounds and a pile of rocks. Perhaps it was an ancient native burial site."

Samuel gaped at De Chaste in disbelief. "But...but what about the cross, sir?"

De Chaste kicked the base of the cross. The impact instantly collapsed a chunk of the cross into a pile of rotted dust. "A remarkable coincidence. Two logs falling on each other into the shape of a cross."

Stunned, Samuel pointed to the rocks behind him. "And the church? And the graveyard over there with the wooden crosses?"

De Chaste shrugged. "All I see here is a mound of rocks, nothing more. By the savages, I see the sticks that look something like crosses. But in reality, it is nothing."

Samuel's cheeks flushed red in exasperation. "Coincidence? Nothing? Sir, I know what this is! This was an Irish settlement! I would stake my reputation as a mapmaker on it!"

De Chaste's eyes narrowed into daggers. "Would you stake your life on it?"

Samuel gasped. "Excuse me, sir?"

De Chaste inched closer. "Why are we here, Samuel? Why did we travel thousands of miles away from our homes and our loved ones? We are here to claim this land for the King of France, to map its boundaries and to begin the process of colonization. This land will become New France, a glorious extension of our homeland. It will also allow our fellow countrymen a chance to immigrate to a land of plenty in which they can begin new and challenging lives.

"Now what do you think would happen if you

returned home with these outrageous stories of ancient Celtic habitations that perhaps existed hundreds of years ago? Do you think France would still have the legal right to colonize this land? Are you willing to jeopardize our future claim because you have let your imagination run wild while looking at a pile of sticks and rocks?"

De Chaste lowered his voice to a growl. "The King himself has given me strict orders to ensure that the claiming and mapping of this land for France goes smoothly and as planned. Do not force me to mention your wild fairy tales of an Irish settlement to His Majesty when we return. I understand he will execute anyone he feels represents a threat to his plans of expansion."

De Chaste put a hand on Samuel's shoulder, his voice now becoming more fatherly.

"Samuel, look around at this sight with new eyes. This is nothing more than, at most, a native burial ground. You do see that now, don't you?"

De Chaste bent down and picked up the disturbed vines. He used them once again to conceal the wooden cross. Samuel stood and watched his commander, still dumbfounded by what he had just heard. De Chaste straightened and looked Samuel right in the eye.

"I didn't hear you. What do you now see when you look around?"

Samuel swallowed as he surveyed the area. "I... I see piles of rocks and sticks. It's nothing more than a native burial site."

De Chaste patted him on the back. "Good for you. You have a bright future, Samuel de Champlain.

Don't throw it all away on several mounds of dirt."

"Yes, sir."

"When we arrive at the ship," De Chaste continued, "I want you to find a dozen of the thickest clods in the crew. It's a full moon this evening. Return here tonight by skiff with some pick-axes and shovels. Do a little rearranging of the stones and dirt mounds so that no one else comes to the same silly conclusion that you somehow arrived at. Understood?"

"Yes, sir," said Samuel, defeat permeating his voice.

De Chaste marched back to the warriors, leaving Samuel standing alone beside the cross. The warriors, hearing the approach of the commander, stood up and followed him down the path. Samuel crouched down and removed the vines one last time, gazing at the ancient beauty of its design. He knew that by the end of the night, the cross would remain only in his memory. Sweeping his hand along the cross, he suddenly noticed under the wood a small, rectangular stone with a crude inscription. Amazingly, it was a rounded headstone with a Celtic inscription.

"Here Lies Kiera, Devoted Wife and Loving Mother."

Unable to decipher the entire inscription, he managed to sound out the name at the top.

"Kiera."

Samuel de Champlain allowed his fingers to retrace the etching of the name before he bowed his head in shame.

"Forgive me, Kiera, for what I am about to do."

AUTHOR'S NOTE

In *Stolen Away*, I have attempted to bring to life the story of a people whose blood stains one of the darkest chapters of Canadian history. Genocide was committed against the Beothuck nation by English settlers throughout the eighteenth century. When the English arrived in Newfoundland, they built their first encampments within the handful of sheltered bays that contained an abundance of fish and wild game. Of course, those same bays were also the summer residences of the Beothuck people. The Beothuck were a generous nation and they were willing to share the resources of their island with the newcomers. Unfortunately, the British were not as hospitable to the Beothuck.

The clash between two very different cultures became the flashpoint for one of the most gruesome episodes in North American history. The British, with superior weapons, forced the Beothuck out of their vital summer hunting, fishing and egg gathering sites. Retreating inland, the starving Beothuck were left with only two choices: suffer from malnutrition in the resource-poor interior, or steal from the newcomers. Soon, the British discovered that their drying meat, sealskins and fishing nets were being stolen from the villages in the dead of night.

The British retaliated with sickening coldness. Hunting down the Beothuck summer camps one by one, armed British thugs executed entire villages, first by shooting Beothuck men and women in cold blood, then rounding up the remaining terrified children and slitting all of their throats. Finally, the native camps were looted of their food and pelts, leaving the torched mamateeks to burn to the ground. There are even stories of skilled French and Mi'kmaq bounty hunters being brought to Newfoundland to hunt down the Beothuck, with the reward of twenty pounds for each Beothuck killed, regardless of age. By 1827, the last of the Beothuck, a captured young woman who had been taken to St. John's, died of tuberculosis. Her name was Shananditti (this young woman should not be confused with Shawnadit, the young female character from my story who had a similarly tragic life).

Before her death, Shananditti gave us a glimpse of Beothuck culture. Although she was not able to learn the English language, she willingly drew pictures of her beliefs and how her family of seventy-two members, when she was first born, managed to live off the land. She also illustrated the cold-blooded murders, by local English hunters, of her aunts, uncles, cousins, mother and father. Her entire family was destroyed within the short twenty-seven years of her life.

It is hard to believe that such a crucial part of Canadian history has been successfully erased from our school textbooks. Who were the Beothuck? They did not have a written language, so their extensive oral history has been lost forever. Did they have contact with the Vikings? There is archeological evidence proving that the Beothuck mastered iron forging technology well before the arrival of Columbus, the only First Nation in the Americas to do so. Did the Vikings pass this technology onto the Beothuck?

Were ancient Irish mariners also successful at crossing the North Atlantic, and did they have contact with the Beothuck? Shananditti explained in her drawings how the Beothuck feared a devil-like entity, making the Beothuck one of the few First Nations to have such a Christian-like concept of good and evil. Due to the brutality of the early European settlers, we will never know the full story of the Beothuck nation. Lost forever is the knowledge and wisdom of a First Nation that existed at the crucial cultural crossroad between Europe and North America.